Kookie Dough

Jacobs Brothers

2

Bella Jay

JACOBS BROTHERS #2

BELLA JAY

First paperback edition August 2025
ISBN 978-1-967935-02-4

www.authorbellajay.com

To my readers who love them a whole lot of spice.

The Playlist

I love me a good playlist! Get into the musical vibes I felt that related to Yadah & Nelly's story.

Scan for the playlist on Spotify.

Bellaverse Glossary

Welcome to the Bellaverse!

The world is always growing, and here's what you need to know for this book:

- **Places**
  - **Luminique:** A tropical haven with stunning beaches, lush hills, and vibrant culture. It's known for its relaxed atmosphere, rich history, and delicious cuisine, offering both adventure and laid-back vibes.
  - **Southgate:** A major metropolitan city surrounded by smaller cities and neighborhoods. Think of it as the Atlanta of the Bellaverse.
  - **Bexley:** A small town about two hours north of Southgate, tucked in the mountains.

Cookie Dough By 'Definition'...

Cookie Dough | The Food - The thing about raw cookie dough is that you know you shouldn't eat it, but you can't resist licking the bowl clean or at least a spoon. It's a risk worth taking.

Cookie Dough | The Strain - A sensational high. Euphoric. Fucking magic. An instant high. It hits hard. It hits fast. It hits everywhere. *! Warning* - can be overwhelming and will give you the munchies.

Chapter 1
Yadah

"How much do you wanna bet he's only fine from behind?" Dale, my co-worker turned closest friend, said from beside me. "But damn, what a behind it is."

My eyes moved from my phone, where I was trying to pull up our hotel information, to Dale, whose eyes were glued to someone a few feet ahead of us. I barely laid eyes on the man before going back to what I was doing. "I know your mama raised you better than to judge people."

"Now you know that ungrateful hoe ain't want shit to do with me, but Johnny told me to mind my business. I never listened."

"I see."

"But am I wrong? Look at him. Tall. Golden brown skin. Nice clothes— fresh off a plane? That's strike number one that he's ugly. Because if he had a long flight like us… ain't nobody got time to dress that good. There's no way he's fine from the front. If he is, he probably got a vienna sausage." I snickered. Leave it to Dale to analyze someone. "Let me go throw this in the trash," he said, shaking his empty water bottle before leaving my side.

My eyes peeked back up at the *fine-from-behind* specimen to see him looking to his left, and the immediate thump in my yoni told me something my brain already knew. He was not ugly by a long shot.

"So," I dragged out when Dale returned. "You're telling me, a man can't be tall, have a good physique from behind, nice booty, beautiful skin… and can't have a cute face?"

"I mean, they can. But either he gay or just too fucking fine. And I'm hoping he's gay, actually."

I snorted because I should have known his fast tail was plotting. "I hate to burst your bubble, but he was chatting it up with the girl next to him while you were gone. And he can't be that ugly because she's pretty cute."

"You right about her being cute. Sis out here a whole seven at the airport, which means she probably a solid ten when she take the time. Damn," Dale sighed. "But he could still be ugly with money, so that makes him worth it."

"Why are you always looking for men everywhere we go?" I asked through giggles.

"'Cause I'm hella single, and I like to get my peen wet."

"Obviously."

"You have your fun over there with that old guy who be between your legs, and I'll spend my time finding people's sons to ruin."

"Wow," I chuckled. "Well, how about this? You owe me a drink if he is cute. And if he's not, first round of drinks on me."

"Well, you know I'ma take that chance, so how we about to figure this out?"

"Follow my lead." I wrapped my hand around my suitcase handle and moved towards the definitely *fine-all-around* specimen. "Excuse me," I tapped his shoulder. As soon as his eyes landed on my face, the sides of his lips started to turn up. "You're Deuce the Almighty's brother, aren't you?" I mentioned his brother who was an NBA star.

His smile widened. "And you're X's friend."

I rolled my eyes playfully. "It's Yadah."

"I know."

We shared a chuckle at our standard greeting to one another as he wrapped his arms around me. It was an inside joke that had started almost three years ago.

Kookie Dough

When my eyes landed on Dale behind him, he was gawking, and I was sure he was cursing me out in his head. Clearly, Jonel Jacobs was no stranger to me. He was my best friend's, Kristmas — or X as he and his brothers called her — brother-in-law. Not to mention, we grew up in the same small town together. Though back in those days, Nelly did not make my yoni thump on sight.

And because he was damn near four years younger than me, I definitely wasn't checking for him. But damn, if God didn't bless him and his brothers in the looks department. I couldn't help but wonder if that trickled down to the nether region. However, I had no plans to ever find out.

"Krissy ain't tell me you were getting in a couple of days early as well," I said, pulling back.

"I hadn't planned on it but said fuck it. I need as much of a vacation as possible."

"That must mean business is going well." Nelly knew how to throw down in a kitchen, which made it even harder to resist his ass because if there was one thing I loved, it was eating good food. He had his own restaurant in Southgate, and from what Kristmas had told me, Nelly's 101 was becoming the *it* spot.

"Yeah, that's one thing I can't complain about. By the way, Tiffani," he grabbed the attention of the pretty, light, golden-brown chick beside him. Her loose, pretty brown curls, that I thought might've been a nice ass wig from afar, made me think she had to have some kind of Hispanic blood in her. "This is Yadah, X's best friend."

"Nice to meet you, girl," she said with a heavy accent that made me think she was not only Hispanic, but she also had to be from one of the boroughs of New York. "We about to turn the fuck up!" She did a little dance that made all of us laugh.

"I know that's fucking right," Dale said, dropping into the conversation before I could introduce him. "Since my friend is rude, I'm Dale, y'all. Her plus one."

"Boy, you ain't give me a chance." I rolled my eyes as they greeted him.

"Babe," Tiffani said, "I think that's our ride."

"Bet. Y'all got a way to the hotel, or you wanna ride with us?" Nelly asked.

"We do not," I answered, and Dale and I happily followed Nelly and Tiffani to the SUV that was indeed waiting on them.

"You played the fuck out of me, and trust, I'm not gonna forget," Dale whispered to me, and I snorted.

"Aye, you lost fair and square, boo. Run me my drink after we check in."

"Forget you." He grabbed my elbow, slowing me down and putting more space between us and them. "But got damn; he's fine as fuck all around."

Don't I know.

"Where y'all from?" Tiffani asked fifteen minutes into our drive.

"Texas born and raised, baby," Dale spoke first. "But this one," he looked my way, "is from Clampton County, but she came on over to the best place to live ever."

"After New York," Tiffani stated, confirming that she was from where I'd suspected. "But Texas seems fun. You like it?" she asked, looking at me.

"I do. I was ready for something new and different from what I was used to. I got it."

"That's how I felt moving to Southgate, and I love it there. I moved for school…"

The small talk conversation continued with Dale and Tiffani leading the conversations while I took in the scenery. Luminique, was a beautiful island whose culture was easy to see as we drove through the city, heading to the hotel Kristmas had required us to book.

The reason we were here was to celebrate Deuce's, her husband, birthday. I couldn't wait to see my girl because it had been months since we'd last spent time together. The last time I had been able to make it to one of these group shindigs she loved to plan was their one year wedding renewal a year and a half ago.

That was also the last time I had seen Nelly, and it was starting to bother me that every time I saw him, he got finer. Granted, it had only been a couple of times with large gaps in between, but damn, when was he going to settle into his fine and be done?

"Y'all wanna stop?" Nelly's voice brought me back into what was happening around me. Everyone gave their answer, and mine didn't matter because the driver was already pulling off of the road.

"What is this?" I whispered to Dale.

"The driver said some local market that happens once a week, and some cool shit be happening. I wasn't listening, but clearly you weren't either."

"Shut up," I quipped as we clambered out the SUV. I had a tendency to be in my head whether I was alone or with a crowd.

As we entered the entrance of the market, we all paused for a second.

There was so much happening; I didn't know where to look first. All I knew was that this was a true depiction of the culture, and I loved it. "Fresh ass coconut water," I grinned, as my eyes landed on a man chopping up coconuts. I loved coconut.

"Oh, hell yeah," Nelly said from beside me before taking the lead and heading in the direction of what would surely make my morning.

After we all got fresh coconut water, we wandered around the market, and before I knew it, I'd purchased fresh pineapple, mango, lychee, and some other fruit I didn't know the name of, but the fruit stand lady let me try it, and I was sold.

"What's happening over there?" Tiffani pointed to where music was playing, and a slew of people were standing around, vibing out to the music.

"Oh, we gotta go see. Fine men might be over there," Dale stated, and I chuckled at his antics. He was determined to find him a boo, or at least good eye candy, as soon as possible. I couldn't blame him about the eye candy, though I, myself, was still having a difficult time not drooling over Nelly's fine ass with his girl right beside him. And I liked her, so I was trying my damndest to stay respectful.

"Ayeee!" Tiffani exclaimed as we joined the crowd and saw the show the local ladies were putting on. They were doing a synchronized dance that was a whole vibe in itself. The way they were moving their hips was magical, and I was a little bit jealous 'cause I ain't think mine knew how to whip it like that.

One of the women's eyes landed on me, and I froze when she outstretched her arms to me.

"Come, come," she said, pulling me into the center.

"Yes girl, go!" Tiff pushed me forward, and I started laughing to hide my uncomfortableness. I hated being directly in the spotlight, but I loved to dance.

I threw my arms up a little and moved my hips like one of the women instructed me. I snorted as she gassed me up but then screamed in laughter when she grabbed Nelly and pulled him behind me.

"Dance with yo' wife, handsome man," she said in broken English, causing Nelly and I to laugh. Neither one of us wasted our breath trying to explain we weren't together. I hoped Tiffani hadn't heard her, but when I looked to my right, she and Dale were in a groove, laughing as much as Nelly and me at the locals, mistaking them for a couple as well.

"Oh my God!" Tiffani exclaimed as we got out of the SUV at our hotel an hour later. We'd spent the rest of the drive basking in the fun we had at the market in just a short time. "That was one way to be welcomed to a new country. This trip is gonna be one for the books. I feel that shit. And girl, you were moving them hips, chica; I saw you!"

"I might can do a lil' something something with what my mama gave me," I laughed. I loved her vibe. Between her and Dale alone, I saw the trip being exactly what I needed. But add in the Jacobs brothers and my boo, Krissy… this was definitely going to be a classic getaway.

Chapter 2
Nelly

"So, before they get down here," Tiffani said, "what's up with you and Yadah?"

I raised a brow at her question, finishing off my drink as we sat at the bar of our hotel, waiting for Yadah and Dale. Tiffani had invited them to join us for dinner tonight. "What you mean what's up with us? Nothing."

"So, you never smashed?" Tiffani gave me a dumbfounded look that made me chuckle. "Because I woulda smashed."

"Of course your ass would have. You always tryna turn somebody out."

"My tongue is magical, baby; you know that. And trust me, the magic juju works on both men and women."

I shook my head at her. "No," I answered her, "we've never fucked. She's my sister-in-law's best friend."

"What that got to do with anything? You acting like they been together."

"You don't know X like I do. She'll be down my throat, knowing how I am."

"You mean a low-key hoe?"

"Shut the fuck up," I said through laughter. "You still fuck with me, though."

"Maybe I like hoes."

"Or maybe you're no better miss, 'I woulda smashed'."

"That was just a matter of fact statement. And because I'm trying to figure out how y'all got so much chemistry if you've never been between them pretty legs of hers."

"You reaching. We don't have chemistry." We didn't. We barely knew each other. Growing up in Bexley meant that I knew of her, but we weren't in the same grade nor did we frequent the same circles. My brothers and X were the only people we had in common. "It's just a no for me."

"Don't let me find out you're one of them 'Ion like dark-skinned girls' types of dudes."

My brows pulled in because that was the furthest thing from the truth. I was the type of nigga who really didn't discriminate, and my preference was a juicy, tight pussy and a pretty face. Everything else was negotiable.

"Can a nigga just not be interested?" I shot back, making her chuckle. "And if we being honest, Yadah was an ugly duckling growing up."

"Well," Tiff paused to sip her tropical drink, "ain't shit *ugly duckling* about her anymore." She nodded behind me, and I looked over my shoulder to see that she was absolutely right.

Yadah came into my line of view, dressed in an all-white, body-hugging dress that stopped just below her knees. Growing up, Yadah had been a stick figure with a head too big for her body. Let's just say, her body finally caught up to that head of hers, and she looked good.

Okay, she fine as fuck. Still not fucking.

"Sorry, I'm late."

"All good. Where's my new bestie?" Tiff asked.

Yadah rolled her deep, onyx-colored orbs. "Girl, that man already found him a boo. We checked out the beach after we got settled in, and next thing I knew, he had picked up a bae. They doing something tonight, so I got ditched already. This why I shoulda never made him my plus one," she laughed. "But I'm starving, where we going?"

"There's some parking lot vendor shit I heard that goes down a couple blocks from here," I spoke up. "Apparently it be poppin'."

And it was.

We heard the music before we could fully see the sight we were walking up on. It reminded me of an outdoor food truck festival I'd seen in Southgate mixed with the vibe of a club let out.

"Y'all," Tiff grabbed our attention. "I'm two seconds from moving here. This looks lit."

"Right," Yadah agreed as we all trudged deeper into the mix of things. After twenty minutes, we had settled on one of the food trucks and grabbed a table to eat our food.

"The men here are fine, fine. And them French accents — goodness gracious," Yadah said, and of course, Tiffani's ass agreed.

"Y'all not gonna be oogling over men like the finest one ain't in your presence."

"But you don't speak French, so you're null and void," Yadah said with a wink.

I never felt like I could get a full read on Yadah, and I knew that was half of the reason I never gave her a second thought. There were times when she was shy, quiet, and a little modest. And then, there were times when she was bold, carefree, and flirtatious.

I didn't know who she was deep down, and I didn't like to dig.

"I want you," Tiffani gassed me up. "But if—"

"Shut up, T," I cut her off, and they both shared a laugh at my expense. I was definitely gonna make Tiffani's ass pay for that later, but for now, I'd let her be great.

"HELL NO," I SANG, FINISHING OFF MY DRINK. "THAT SHIT IS WEAK. HOW the fuck I look, telling a woman she hurt my feelings?"

"See, that's just some pride nonsense," Yadah said, shaking her head. "It's not weak."

"I mean," Tiff countered, "if he talking about, 'you hurt my feelings because you ain't kiss me goodnight', then I'ma be like, 'boy, shut yo' ass up."'

"SEE! Weak shit. Fuck that." We all shared a laugh. We'd spent the better part of our time having light debates around random questions Yadah would shoot off between us, vibing out at the *parking lot party*, as we called it. This time, the question had been to me about if I would tell a woman that she hurt my feelings.

No. Fuck that.

"It would be sexy," Yadah shrugged. "To see a man who knew how to express himself and communicate what he's actually feeling."

"I can express myself without being a simp."

She rolled her eyes at me, something I'd come to realize she did at least ten times an hour. I was almost sure it was an automatic response to everything she didn't agree with. I found it cute, though.

Interacting with her outside of how we'd normally done was interesting. Usually, our interactions were in larger group settings with my brothers, their significant others, and other family and friends. It was never this intimate where I could study her more.

"And that's that male pride and ego talking," Yadah countered.

"It's not. It's deeper than that."

"Is it, though?" She scrunched up her face.

I smirked, sitting up straighter.

"Oh lord, here he go, thinking he Dr. Phil or something," Tiff commented, and I flipped her off.

"Here's what y'all women don't get...no one cares about men's feelings, so we just gotta eat that hurt. Meditate and smoke a joint."

"We do care, and that's really some sad shit to say," Yadah countered.

I shrugged. "You telling me that you and your friends wouldn't have a great ass time roasting a nigga who told you 'you hurt my feelings'?"

"To be honest, depending on the situation — I might not even tell my friends. And IF I did, they may laugh in context, but then they're going to ask for the full story, and if I was wrong, they'd drag me. Not him."

"Then, the women you associate with are different. Not the majority. Regardless, with men, our thought process is that we don't wanna show too much weakness or allow folks to peep what hurts us because it can be used against us."

"Sounds like pride and ego once again," Tiffani chimed in. "Get over yourselves."

"Like I already said, it ain't, but we can agree to disagree."

After a few more friendly debates, Yadah called it a night, while Tiff and I finished off a couple more drinks and enjoyed the scene.

"That was fun." Tiffani intertwined her hand in mine as we started our walk back to the hotel. "I'm happy I kept you around so I can be your plus one to things like this."

I paused, placing my hand on her back and pulling her closer into me. "You've been saying little slick shit all night." I gave her a kiss. "You know you're about to pay."

She licked her lips. "Sí papi, I do. Which makes it all the more fun." She winked, and we started back in stride.

"You and Yadah hit it off," I said as the hotel came into view. "Ganging up on me and shit. Wait until my brothers get here; we bringing all them questions back up."

She giggled. "We did. And I'm still confused on how or why you ain't smash."

The sides of my mouth curved up. "What's wrong with me just not trying to take it there?"

She shrugged. "Nothing really. But you're telling me, if she was offering up the goods, you'd turn her down?"

"I ain't tryna fuck versus would I fuck if it's offered up on a platter, are two different things."

"I bet they are," she said as we walked into the hotel lobby.

"Tiff, if you tryna smash, shoot your shot. Don't be tryna pressure me," I laughed, cutting through her bullshit. She'd been riding Yadah's non-existent dick all day, and we both knew why. So, she might as well leave me out of this.

"I mean," she sang, pushing the button for the elevator. "I thought *we all* coulda had a little fun, but we missed our chance, clearly."

"Yo fault." Tiffani and I had had our share of threesomes, so for her to be putting the idea on the table didn't surprise me at all. That was one reason why I fucked with her and tended to invite her as my plus one to things like this. She was chill, fun, and liked to fuck. My kind of woman.

"There's always..." Her voice trailed off as the elevator door opened.

"Oh!" Yadah said, noticing us. "Y'all left. Damn. I was about to head back over because apparently, my room is in use," she frowned.

"Okay then, Dale!" Tiff said, snapping her fingers.

"I hate him," Yadah groaned. "Are y'all heading up, though?"

"Yeah," Tiffani said. "Wanna join us for a night cap? We have liquor and edibles."

THIS SHIT IS HILARIOUS.

Tiffani was clearly out of her league with this one. She had been subtly flirting with Yadah, who was super oblivious to all of the shots Tiff kept making and missing. I was enjoying the show, but I was about to call it a night soon because it didn't seem like Tiffani was going to ask for what she wanted from Yadah directly, and the weight of traveling was starting to set in on me.

"I think I gotta pee," Yadah announced, suddenly. I snickered at her. Her high had kicked in, and since then, she'd made it a point to let us know what she was about to do or thought she wanted to do.

"Go pee, chica." Tiff slapped her on the thigh, bottom lip pulled in, and eyeing her with a look I knew all too well.

Yadah giggled, pulled herself together, and danced her way to the bathroom. One thing I'd managed to observe about her today, she loved to dance. And I didn't mind watching her sway her hips.

Licking my lips, I moved my eyes from the bathroom door that was closing behind Yadah to Tiffani as she groaned, falling down on the king-sized bed.

"You know she has no idea you're flirting with her."

"Shut up, Jonel. I wasn't trying to come on too aggressive. You know how I can be."

I chortled. "I do. If you want her, tell her 'cause she's not taking your *way-too-fucking* subtle bait."

"It'd be easier if I could get a read on her." She propped herself up on her elbows, her pretty brown curls falling all around her face. Tiffani was definitely something great to look at, and like me, she was used to getting what she wanted. "Do you honestly think she'd be down for some *fun* with us? Or should I just drop—" She snapped her mouth shut when the bathroom door swung open.

"I think I need water," Yadah stated. I smirked because she could've been talking to us or just speaking aloud. "Yeah, water." She started towards the kitchenette.

"Y'all wanna play a game?" I asked, causing Yadah to turn around towards me as she guzzled back the water.

"What game?"

"Truth or Dare."

She rolled her eyes. I had to admit, while she'd been high, she hadn't rolled them as much. "I haven't played that in years, and the last time I did, people started getting wild. What are the other options?"

"What's wrong with things getting a," Tiff positioned her thumb and pointer finger close together, "little wild? We're all grown and consenting adults." Yadah's brows knitted together, as if she was contemplating what to say next. "Come on, Yaya," Tiff said seductively, "it'll be fun. Scared you're gonna get asked to kiss a girl?" She winked, and if Yadah had missed all of Tiff's signs before, the way her slitted eyes opened wider led me to believe she caught that one.

Yadah's mouth parted, closed, parted again, and nothing came out.

"If you've never kissed a girl before, I promise I don't bite." Tiff was going for the gold, finally. *Subtle Tiff* had left the building.

Yadah snickered. "I've kissed a girl before. College," she shrugged. I low-key hated that I couldn't pinpoint if I was or wasn't surprised by that revelation.

"Well see, you're not that innocent."

"You thought I was?"

"More innocent than me at least, but that's what truth or dare is for. So, we playing or not?"

"Let's play, but I'm opting out of any dares that I don't like." Yadah glanced my way, and I smirked. Little did she know, I was an innocent bystander in all of this. "Me first. Nelly, truth or dare?"

"Truth." I licked my lips.

"How many times have you had sex in your restaurant?"

I smirked and held up a zero.

"You're lying!" she shot back.

"My restaurant is sacred to me. If I ever corrupt someone's daughter in there, she had better be my wife or someone I plan to make my wife."

"Which means it's never gonna happen 'cause someone has long term commitment issues," Tiff added in.

"I don't, but we not about to get into that, *pot*." She snickered at my comment. "Now, truth or dare?"

We kept things light and fun for the first two rounds.

Tiffani told us about one of her worst sex experiences and on a dare ran up and down the hallway twice in just her underwear.

Yadah revealed she'd never had a threesome and on a dare flashed us her pretty ass titties.

And when it was back to me, Yadah dared me to give Tiffani a lap dance to "Baby Shark", which had us all dying of laughter.

"My turn!" Tiffani sang. "Truth or dare, Yaya?"

Yadah pulled her mouth to the side. "Dare."

Tiff ran her tongue over her lips. "I dare you," she paused smirking, "to let me eat you out."

Okay, shit. Round three was coming in hot.

Yadah's eyes grew, and I held back my chuckle. Confusion mixed with curiosity covered her face, which made my dick come alive at the thought of what might happen next.

Yadah was a wild card.

She giggled, "Tiff you're crazy. Nelly, get your girl. I'm too high for this." Another giggle. One of those, *did she really say what I think she said?* type of giggles.

I held up my hands. "I'm not in this. But," I shrugged, "a dare *is* a dare."

"You would say that."

I chuckled.

"But regardless of my answer, don't think this is about to be the moment I check threesome off of my non-existent bucket list. I'm not sleeping with you." She pointed her finger at me as if she was accusing me of a crime.

"Trust me, I'm not asking you to. I'm just here for moral support and to watch *if* you accept the dare. *And* if that's cool. Otherwise, I can leave." That was a fact. As much as I would not have minded taking part — because *pussy times two* — I'd settle for the show. If she wasn't cool with that, I'd see myself out 'cause one thing I wasn't about was being somewhere I wasn't wanted.

"Leave her be, Nelly. I was just trying to spice things up. See how *wild* we could get. Give her an experience to remember. But if you not down for it…"

Silence consumed the room as Yadah fiddled with her hands. The look on her face told me she was about to say—

"I'm going to need another shot."

Oh, that's not what I thought.

Tiff's face held the same expression as mine — shock. "Is that a yes to the dare?"

"Yes, but after you eat me out, that's it. I'm not—"

"Shh," Tiff put a finger up to her mouth. "This is all about you. I got him for anything else I need. Let's have some fun. I'll get you that shot, and you strip for me."

Yadah stood frozen.

I was waiting for her to change her mind, but instead, she reached behind herself and tried to unzip her dress.

"Need some help?" I offered and expected her to tell me to fuck off, but instead, she walked into my space.

I stood as she turned away from me. With her this close, I could really take in how stunning her brown skin was. As much as I wanted to run my hands down her bare shoulders to see if she was as smooth as butter, I didn't.

"Here, beautiful." Tiffani handed her a double shot of a specialty liquor we got while at the market. "I'll be right back," she said, heading to the bathroom.

Besides the music, the only thing that could be heard was the zipper as it slid down her back. "You good?" I asked. "If you don't wanna do this, just say that shit now."

As her almost bare back and lace thong came into view, my dick danced, thinking he was about to come out to play. *Nah playa, we gotta take one for the team tonight.*

"One thing about me, Jonel, is that I'm not easily persuaded. I'm just curious as to why you're okay with letting your girl please me if you can't join in."

I was glad she kept her eyes ahead and wasn't taking note of me loving the view of the dip where her ass met her back.

"I mean," I leaned into her ear as my hands landed on her waist, gingerly pulling her into me. "If you saying you want me to join in—"

She chuckled, pulling away from my hold and glancing over her shoulder. "You might be too young to handle me, but you can stay and enjoy the show however you please."

I wanted to rebut, but my dick had already snitched on me, and I was positive she felt it against her ass before she moved.

The bathroom door opened.

She winked and let her dress drop to the ground. It was at that point I should have known she was way more of a tease than I gave her credit for.

I dropped back in my chair, smirked, and grabbed my drink. *Showtime.*

Chapter 3
Yadah

rug Abuse Resistance Education.

D.A.R.E failed me.

Because had it not, I wouldn't be high off my ass, about to let some chick eat me out while Nelly's *way too fucking fine ass* watched.

I know what I said to him. I know what bold words came out of my mouth, but I was nervous as fuck.

But also turned the hell on.

I didn't know if it was the weed, liquor, or the excitement that a woman wanted to bury her head between my legs without me having to do nothing but enjoy the orgasmic high — but whatever it was, had me wet.

I was a sucker for head.

A certified headhunter.

I was the type that would take bomb head over bomb penis any day if I had to choose. At twenty-seven, it had been such a job to find a man who could make me orgasm vaginally at least eighty percent of the time, that it seemed like an easy decision to pick head over penis.

So, if Tiffani wanted to suck me dry, I was going to allow it.

I just wasn't sure if I was going to enjoy it as much as I was trying to convince myself I would.

"Relax," Tiff hummed in my ear before she trailed kisses down my jaw line until our lips met. As we kissed, she guided me down onto the bed, and I wondered if she could hear my heart beating through my chest.

I heard it.

It got louder once she moved her lips from my mouth down to my neck, down my stomach, and to between my thighs. She paused to remove my panties, and my eyes landed on her relishing in what was hidden between my legs.

She wasted no time diving in, and I was glad she wasn't trying to do the most. Just get to the main event.

I closed my eyes to relax and be in the moment. I imagined the person I wanted between my legs and simultaneously cursed myself.

"Fuck," I groaned as Tiff stuck two fingers inside of me, and then her mouth gripped down on my clit.

"Mhmm," Tiffani moaned.

I pulled my bottom lip deep into my mouth as my eyes opened, and my head dropped to the side.

My eyes landed on Nelly.

Same spot we'd left him in, but now… he had his dick in his hand.

He smirked, sipped from the drink in his other hand, and continued running his palm up and down his shaft.

I couldn't look away.

I had felt his manhood against my ass, but seeing it was a different story.

That shit he was holding was a first-place trophy.

Pretty and dripping in gold. Long, juicy, and mesmerizing.

He was ten feet away, and I still could see the details of it.

Maybe being high gave me supersonic eyesight because there's no way in hell his penis was that fucking pretty.

A hot, tingling sensation rushed through me as my eyes met his.

They were intense as he watched Tiff devour me.

Or maybe he was watching me, *watching him*, again.

It wasn't until he mouthed, 'You better cum' or maybe it was, 'You gonna cum?' that I realized it was me. It didn't matter what the exact words were because my mind registered the 'you' and 'cum' just fine.

It could have been a statement. A request. Or a question.

However, my body took it as a direct command and ran with it, and I exploded into Tiff's mouth.

"Fuck yes," she hummed, sucking up my juices. The trembling in my legs refused to stop, and my eyes couldn't seem to stop staring at him.

I squeezed them shut and threw my head back as the orgasm continued to flow through me, and Tiffani applied pressure.

"Shit," I hissed.

"Damn, chica," Tiff said, coming up for air. "I suspected that you were going to taste good, but I see you take real good care of this pretty punani of yours."

I laughed, rolling onto my side, thinking she was done and trying to stop the thumping of my yoni — and not for Tiffani. For Jonel fucking Jacobs.

Fuck. Fuck. Fuck.

I wanted him to join us.

All that shit talking I had done, and I wanted him — and his beautiful dick — on this side of the room.

To make the fantasy that was supposed to stay a fantasy, a reality.

Fuck.

Tiffani rubbed my thigh. "You tapping out?"

"Oh, I thought," I looked at her, "you were done."

A seductive smile danced on her lips, "Oh, baby, trust me. I can definitely keep putting on a show for our audience."

Nelly's baritone as he laughed only made the sensations in my stomach go berserk. "I'm all for an encore presentation." I forced my eyes to look at him. His dick was tucked back away, but his pants were still unzipped, and I imagined that the bear was just one poke from being back woke. "Unless, you want to do something else."

The way his thick, pink tongue glided over his lips, I knew what he was insinuating.

But I was not going to give into wanting him just yet.

I turned onto my back and pulled Tiffani into my space. I outlined her lips with my tongue and then planted a soft kiss on her pink lips.

"I want," my head turned towards Nelly, "you to please her while she continues to please me."

"Look who's calling the shots. I like it," Tiff gassed me up before kissing me again. She was a different breed of woman, and I loved it. I didn't know what kind of relationship they had going on, but I had come to the executive decision that for tonight, that was none of Kayadah Kookman's business.

I looked out of my peripheral to see that Nelly was already making his way towards us. As Tiff positioned herself back between my legs, he stripped out of his pants and top. I watched his every move and couldn't believe how turned on I was just from his presence.

Ever since I laid eyes on Nelly almost three years ago and saw that he was no longer some cute little boy I didn't give a second look to, I wanted him.

But I also didn't.

He was cocky as fuck, exuded big dick energy, way too damn blunt, and most importantly, younger than me. I knew it wouldn't ever go anywhere, and I had become accustomed to liking my men to come with a little baggage.

Nelly was just not *it*, and I think we both knew it.

But tonight, if nothing else, I was going to ride his face.

"You want me to fuck her or eat her out?" he questioned. His beautiful, light brown eyes bore into me, and my stomach clenched.

"Fuck her from behind." I gasped from the impact of Tiffani's tongue going deeper into me as if she was consenting to the request.

Nelly nodded. He disappeared from my eyesight, and when he returned, he was completely naked. His pretty trophy dick stood at attention as he dropped a handful of condoms on the bed and then put one on.

I was so damn high, I couldn't fully comprehend if I was truly watching him as hard as I thought I was, but I just couldn't stop. The more I took in his every movement, the hotter my body got, and I couldn't let that feeling go.

He positioned himself behind Tiff, and she moaned in delight against me when he entered her.

"Mmmh," Tiff groaned again, arching her back to meet Nelly's strokes while never missing a beat between my legs. Her grips tightened around my hips as I positioned myself on my elbows.

I needed the perfect angle to watch him as he drilled her.

He moved in and out of her vigorously and with such technique that it was nothing short of entertaining and satisfying to watch. When he slowed his pace and leaned forward, she growled and took out his torture on her, on me. My hands gripped the sheets as her tongue buried itself deep into me.

My eyes still hadn't left him.

I had never been so turned on by a man who wasn't even touching me.

And when he did… I became completely undone from a simple touch.

His left hand kept a taunt grip on Tiffani while his right toyed with my nipple.

My nipples were a trigger point, directly tied to my pulsating clit, so it didn't take much of his teasing to send me into oblivion.

"Oh fuck!" I screamed out as a hard orgasm ripped through me from the intensity of what they both were doing to me. His hand went from my nipple to my hand as he allowed me to use his hand for support as if I was giving birth to the orgasm.

And the way it gushed through me, I was sure I had.

I gently pushed Tiff's head back and was thankful when Nelly wrapped his hand around her throat and pulled her back into him. While he continued his assault on her pussy, I slowly rolled onto my side, trying to gather the pieces of me that had escaped with that orgasm.

Tiffani spit out a slew of Spanish curse words, and I looked over my shoulder to see her taking his trophy dick like a certified porn star.

"Throw that fucking ass back," he demanded, and I was no longer surprised by the jump my pussy made. His commands just made me want to do things, and they weren't even directed at me.

This was the type of dangerous sexual energy I had only read about in books.

He pushed down on Tiffani's back as he switched the rhythm of his strokes.

"Fuck me, baby," she cooed. He leaned over, planted a kiss on the side of her face, and when he leaned up, his eyes landed on me.

"Come kiss me," he told me.

I floated over to him without question. When I got close enough, he snatched me to him, and his lips attacked mine. My body was tittering on catching fire just from his request; I was fully ablaze now.

His hand snaked down to between my legs, and a finger slid into me.

Then another.

I moaned against his lips and had no idea how he could navigate kissing and fingering me while still moving in and out of Tiffani.

I couldn't even touch my head and rub my stomach at the same time.

"Shit," Tiffani cursed, and her thigh trembled against mine.

Nelly pulled his lips from mine but kept playing with my bud as he coaxed Tiffani through her orgasm. When she finished, she collapsed on the bed.

"You changed your mind about wanting this dick?" he winked, pulling off the condom soaked with Tiff's juices. He teased me by running a hand up and down the length of his perfect penis.

"No," I lied. From the amused look on his face, he knew I was lying too. "I wanna ride your face, though."

His tongue graced his lips as he crawled onto the bed, hovering over me. His dick tapped against my thigh, and I was tempted to say fuck it and slide it into me. But instead, I asked, "Did you not hear me?"

"Nah, I heard you." He kissed me and flipped us over so that he was on his back, and in one swift movement, he lifted me up by my thighs and sat me on his face. For a black woman, by most standards, I wasn't considered overweight, but he had me thinking my size ten ass was a size two.

I yelped out in pleasure.

His tongue swirled around my pussy lips as he sucked gently, immediately sending quivers through my core.

"Turn around," Tiff requested, sitting up. "I wanna see the faces he makes you make while I ride him."

I maneuvered around just as Tiffani placed a fresh condom on him. She slid down his pole as his tongue assaulted me. *Fuck me.* Tiffani's tongue had been great, once I got past it being attached to a woman, but less than a minute in, and I was ready to drown Nelly. The way his tongue curved through all of the touch points of my most precious place was not normal.

Tiffani leaned forward and grabbed my breasts into her hand. She started sucking on them, and I was almost sure they were both out to kill me and bury my body tonight.

I was kind of okay with it, though.

"Stop holding back," Nelly mumbled, tapping my thigh. I wasn't trying to, but the intense feelings had my body completely lost on what to do.

I leaned forward a little to kiss Tiffani, and what I wasn't expecting was for Nelly's tongue to circle my ass. I chomped down on Tiffani's lip to avoid the scream I wanted to let out from the pleasure that shot through me.

"Let that shit out," she coached. "Soak his face like you did me."

"I ca— FUCK!" I screeched as his tongue applied a type of pressure I wasn't expecting, and my body lost complete control of itself.

Three orgasms later, I tapped out and decided to enjoy the show from beside them.

Tiffani went from riding him to giving him head and I, once again, tried to piece my life back together. I'd never had so many orgasms in one night.

"He's ready for you, boo." Tiffani's voice pulled me out of my orgasmic daze. I turned to see her sitting back on her knees as she ran a hand through her wild hair. "You gonna fuck him to sleep?"

"Nah," Nelly chortled, "she gotta tell me she want the dick first. I need to hear it."

It could've been the weed, but suddenly, I was breathing hard as hell. I definitely did want to feel him, but something deep within me yelled that was a bad idea. *Take the head and move on, girl.*

My low eyes followed Nelly as he got up from the bed. He stalked over to where the bottles of water were and downed one.

"She said I couldn't handle her grown woman pussy." He was

taunting me. "I'll accept the challenge, though. *If* she tells me she wants me."

I rolled my eyes as Tiff whispered into my ear, "No pressure from me, but I highly suggest you experience the D, and if you do, make him pay for making you stroke his ego. Plus," she leaned back as Nelly and his prized possession came back to the bed, "I'd love to watch and be the audience this time." She winked, tapped my thigh, and climbed off of the bed.

I almost felt like I was getting passed around, and I oddly did not mind because I had all of the power. Everything was on my terms, and that turned me on. I could have Nelly sex me to sleep if I wanted to, or I could call it a night. *What did I want and what were the consequences?*

I watched as Tiffani's slender figure sauntered over to where Nelly had been sitting.

The bed fluctuated. My eyes ventured to the beautiful man, and I ate him up like I had been all night. *Shit*, since I saw him at the airport.

"All you gotta do is tell me what you want, and it's yours." As his annoying words came out of his mouth, he hovered over me. He placed a kiss on the right side of my neck then the left, before landing on my lips.

I couldn't help but pull him closer into me, and my body hitched at his penis tapping against my center. "Fucking tell me," he growled mid kiss.

I wish I had the willpower to tease him longer, but I didn't.

I wanted him, *now*.

As deep inside of me as possible.

"I want you," I whispered against his lips. Barely a full second passed before he slid into my warmth that welcomed him with open arms, as if he was a soldier coming home from war.

Nelly groaned and slowly stroked me as if to abuse me for taking so long to admit what I wanted.

The way he fitted within my sacred tunnel was as if my body was the architect that designed his dick.

"Shit," I hissed. The feeling that coursed through me over and over again as he moved in and out of me like a symphony in motion, made me feel like I was on the brink of dissolving. It was as if he was fucking parts of me that had never been discovered.

And I was completely at a loss for words the moment I felt myself already on the verge of an orgasm.

It had never been this easy with *anyone.*

"Fuck, Yadah," he growled, and the way he said my name was just one more layer of intensity. I rotated my hips and matched his strides while begging him not to stop. "This fuckin' pussy."

He slowed for a second and admired himself going in and out of me. His thumb swirled around my clit before his eyes met mine.

I knew we weren't the only ones in the room, however, the way he looked at me made me feel like his dick belonged to me.

It didn't.

It for sure did not with Tiffani ten feet away.

But I was about to take all of it like it did. "What about this pussy?" I questioned. "Worth the tease?"

"Very," he answered without hesitation before switching positions. I was slightly on my side with one leg propped up on his shoulder as he drilled in and out of me so well that I was ready to lose consciousness.

"You gon' tell me when you coming?" he moaned against my ear. "I can feel that shit anyway." I was responding to him in my head, but everything felt so good, the words wouldn't escape my throat. "Cum all over this dick, Yadah," he demanded, and from the way he was pulsating inside of me, I knew he needed me to.

"Fucking make me," I shot back, reaching around to grip his throat.

"Say that shit, again," he begged. "Fuck!" His pace increased.

"Fucking make me, Nelly," I cried as the pressure in my abdomen simmered. "Make me!" I repeated over and over again as he did exactly what I'd asked him to.

His grunts were no match to my screams as he released, and I came harder than I ever had before.

Chapter 4
Nelly

"That looks like Nelly," I heard Dale's voice. I glanced over my shoulder to see him and Yadah. I was happy to see that she wasn't tied to a bed and a trashcan like Tiffani was.

"Yo," I greeted them. "Y'all about to do some island hopping as well?" I pointed behind me to where I was trying to figure out what tour I wanted to buy. All I really wanted to do was spend my day in or near the water to recharge. Between traveling, drinking, getting high, and fucking — my body just needed some sun and relaxation.

"Yeah, but Ackley, my boy toy for the week, family owns a few of these baby yachts. He said he should be able to borrow one since Mondays are slow. You wanna join us? It's us, and we're going to scoop up a couple more of his friends from one of the smaller islands nearby."

"Hell yeah," I said without hesitation. "More privacy is definitely the move."

"Bet. Where's my boo, Tiff?" he asked.

"Man," I dragged out, "she out for the count today. Baby girl woke up this morning and made a beeline for the toilet, and it's been a done deal ever since."

"Damn. What the hell y'all were doing last night to take my friend out like that?" Dale looked between Yadah and me.

"Lots of drinking," Yadah said monotonously. She adjusted her sunglasses, and I wished I could see her eyes. Based on her demeanor, I couldn't quite get a read on her energy towards me.

"She thinks it might've also been what she ate. Either way, she'll be in bed all day."

"Po' tink. I'll turn up for her."

And he wasn't lying.

Dale turned the boat into a mini party boat shortly after we picked up Ackley's friends from the nearby island. The catamaran we were on was nice as fuck and spacious with three cabins. This was the type of boat I could one day see myself sailing around in.

We turned up for the first hour and a half ride to where Ackley had taken us so we could go snorkeling in one of the best spots in the ocean. I had never been snorkeling before, so the shit took my breath away.

After snorkeling, one of Ackley's friends caught us some fish, and we had the freshest seafood I'd ever had.

While everyone continued to party and drink, I chilled on the other side of the boat and soaked up the sun that my body needed. My eyes were closed, but I sensed the presence of someone, and when I cracked open one eye, I saw orange. My tongue ran across my bottom lip as all of Yadah came into view.

We hadn't said much to one another since we got on the boat, and I'd hoped she hadn't let what happened last night get in her head.

I knew she had to have seen me laid out, but as she leaned against the railing of the boat, trying to find her perfect angle to take a selfie, she paid me no mind.

"You want me to take it for you?" I asked, sitting up.

She flinched as if I'd caught her off guard before her eyes met mine. "My bad, did I wake you?" she asked.

"I wasn't sleep." I stood up. "So?"

She pulled her mouth to the side but then outstretched her phone to me. I licked my lips as I watched her get ready for me to take the photos. When the sun hit my brown skin, I looked good. But when that shit pierced down on her above average melanin, dressed in a burnt orange high-waisted bikini, she glistened. *Damn.*

I snapped a few shots at different angles, knowing better than to just take one.

"Lemme see." She held out her hand. "Oh! Okay, then. Let me find out you're secretly a photographer."

I chortled, taking a seat on the couch under the shaded awning. "Nah. Just dated enough women to know it's about the angles."

"It very much is." She plopped down next to me in the shade. I watched as she went through each of the pictures, examining them and immediately yaying or naying them with a quick tap of the delete button.

"What you doing back here?" she asked after a moment. "I completely expected you to be the life of the party, right along with Dale."

"That's 'cause you know me to be that, but that's really just around the people I know. Otherwise, I like to keep to myself. Feel out the vibe first."

"I'm seeing that," she admitted.

"Who you trying to send a message to in the middle of the ocean?" I asked as I watched her click on 'resend' again. There was Wi-Fi on the boat, but it was weak as hell, and all I managed to do was send a text, checking in on Tiffani.

Yadah frowned at me, rolling her eyes per usual. "Someone needs to touch their nose."

I sniggered. "I mean, you got your phone all in my face." It was nowhere near my face, but that was subjective.

"I don't, but if that's the lie you wanna go with, that's fine." She changed angles, so I no longer could be all in her business. I smirked.

"Well, let me rephrase my question. Is who you trying to send them pics to someone who will have a problem with what went down last night?"

Yadah let off a soft chuckle. "It shouldn't," she looked away from me, "Since he's married."

"Oh." I for once couldn't hide my shock.

"Yeah," she said, glancing at me. "I know it's messed up that I'm seeing a married man, but," she shrugged, "I really like him, and I don't know," another shrug, "there's a lot less pressure that comes with dating someone who isn't expecting much from you."

"You don't have to explain yourself to me. I'm not one to judge anyone. But even with the little that I know about you, I will say that I think you deserve someone who isn't someone else's and wants no one but you. And that's coming from someone like me."

"You mean, someone who has threesomes with his girl?"

I smirked. "Tiffani ain't my girl, and even if she was, that would be our business."

She nodded her head. "You right about that. Anyway, I'm probably going to stop seeing him once I get back anyway," she said, and I knew those were just words to get me to change the subject or let the conversation die, so I did.

"Speaking of last night, I did want to make sure everything between us was cool. You were gone by the time I got back from my run this morning."

"Yeah, we're great. Last night was fun, and I didn't do anything I didn't want to. Trust me on that. It was definitely a great way to start this vacation. I was just worried if there was gonna be friction between me and Tiff."

"Nah. Tiff—"

"What y'all back here doing? Not drinking, that's for sure!" Dale's voice made an appearance before he did, cutting into our conversation.

"I think I'm liquored out," Yadah said, and I had to agree. I'd had a couple of shots when we first got things going, but I wasn't in the mood to really drink today.

"Boooo!" he sang, and she laughed at him. "All good, though. But look, I got a proposition for y'all. Ackley wants to know if y'all would be down for sleeping on the boat tonight. He knows this little cove area we can go to anchor at. We'll take the cabin suite, and y'all can have the other two rooms."

"What about his friends?" Yadah asked.

"We're gonna drop them back off and have dinner on that island.

He mentioned that there's a couple of shops we can pick up clothing to sleep in if you need it."

"Y'all already have this shit figured out, so who am I to say no?" I joked.

"What he said," Yadah agreed. "YOLO, right?"

"Exactly, boo! But cool, I'll let my little bae know."

"At least when we get off the boat, you can find better Wi-Fi to send them thirst traps," I said once we were alone again.

Yadah whipped her head my way. "Shut up, Nelly!" She slapped me on my bicep, giggling. I was a little surprised she didn't roll them pretty eyes of hers. A little disappointed.

"Aye, watch your hands, Kooks. Just 'cause you older than me don't mean you can abuse my ass."

"Kooks?" she balled up her face.

"Short for Kookman. Or do you not know your last name?"

"A ha ha," she shot back. "You and your brothers love making up nicknames."

"And the women we do it for tend to love it too. Stop acting like you don't like it."

"'Cause I don't."

"That's too bad. I mean, I could go back to calling you X's friend, but after last night, we past that now."

She hid her face as she shook it, hiding a smile before standing up. "Jonel, go to hell. Respectfully."

"I LAID OUT FRESH TOWELS FOR YOU TWO IN YOUR ROOMS," ACKLEY SAID. "Do you need anything else?" We were anchored for the night in the middle of nowhere, and it was the most peaceful shit ever.

"No," Yadah and I said in unison. "Thanks, Ackley."

"No problem. See you in the morning."

"Good night, y'all!" Dale yelled before their cabin door closed.

I let Yadah shower first, and by the time I emerged from the bathroom, I expected her to be asleep, but she wasn't.

"Night owl?" I asked, poking my head into her cabin to find her laid out on the bed. The shirt she had on did nothing to cover her ass that was barely being hidden by the tiny bikini bottom she'd found at one of the markets.

"Sometimes, but I think my sleep pattern is just messed up. Plus, all of them off and on naps I took today is catching up with me."

"Same. My ass is wide awake. I was thinking about heading back up to the deck to smoke under the stars." Her eyes narrowed at me. I held up a joint I'd rolled while she was in the shower.

"I thought y'all only had edibles."

"I actually just got this while we were at dinner. One of Ackley's friends hooked me up."

She shook her head, smiled, and then nibbled on her bottom lip. Her lips were so juicy; the sight made my dick jump. "Give me a minute, and I'll meet you up there."

Two hours later, and I was enjoying her laughter as it tickled my ear. We were talking about some of the most random shit that we both loved and hated about growing up in a small ass town.

Bexley would forever be home, but once I got out and saw what big city life was like, I couldn't imagine going back to something like it.

"Okay, I need you to be one hundred with me," she said, after composing herself again.

"When am I not?"

"This is true," she said, through laughs. "But is Tiff really sick? Or did she just feel a way after last night?"

"Nah. She really out for the count. And she gon' be upset when she find out I got to spend more time with you today." She took the joint from me, took in a pull, and immediately started coughing and laughing.

"Shit." She fanned herself.

"You don't smoke much, huh?"

"Is it that obvious?"

"A little bit. And that's coming from someone who doesn't smoke a lot either."

"Well, hush up," she sassed. "So," she looked my way. The moonlight was hitting her at the perfect angles. "Have you enjoyed spending time with me?"

The side of my mouth curled up after I exhaled the smoke. "So much so that I'm interested in knowing if you wanna let me fuck you all night."

Even in the darkness of the night, I saw the blood drain from her face at my revelation. "You're so blunt."

I shrugged. "It's my best and worst quality with women."

"Is Tiffani gonna have a problem with you sexing me all night? I just don't want to have no drama on this trip."

"So, you're considering it?"

"Answer the question."

"Just like you and ol' married boy ain't tied to one another, neither are me and Tiff. Like I told you, we not together." She stared at me. "And I don't have no reason to feed you bullshit if that's what you thinking in that head of yours."

"I'm not. You're too blunt to lie."

I sniggered. She had no idea of how blunt I could be, but I'd gotten better at toning it down and not saying the first thing that came to mind in my adult life.

"Okay. Well, all I'm saying is that we're both single, on a mini yacht, in the middle of the ocean… why not take advantage?"

I filled up my lungs with more smoke as she seemed to contemplate my words in her head.

She pulled her bottom lip in. "This would be a shame to waste." The sides of my lips curled up at what sounded like a yes. "Let's go to my room." She went to stand, and I stopped her while putting out the joint.

"I would rather watch you cum under the stars. At least for the first round." Lust filled her eyes as I positioned her onto my lap. Her thick thighs held me in place as I pulled the top she was wearing over her head.

Her lips attacked mine while my hand snaked down her stomach to her center. She let out a light moan against my mouth once I stuck a finger inside of her. She was so damn moist that my dick went from fifty percent hard to one hundred and ten in five seconds.

I stuck another finger into her, stretching her out a little so that she could slide down on me with ease.

After last night, I had to admit, I couldn't wait for her to ride the hell out of me on this boat.

"Take these off." I pulled at the bikini bottoms. I didn't want anything prohibiting me from grabbing every inch of her ass.

She did as I requested, and moments later, she had my dick tautly in her hand while she slowly lowered herself down onto it. Her head fell back as her warmth consumed me. My eyes closed as she adjusted herself to my length.

"Ride this dick."

"How you want me to ride it?" she hummed.

"Like it's yours."

When I opened my eyes, she was smirking at me, and I knew she had accepted the challenge with this lethal ass pussy between her legs.

She rotated her hips into me and then away from me, finding a rhythm. "Fuck, like that," I gritted when she started moving in circles while I moved her hips the way I wanted them to.

"Shit!" she yelped, immediately covering her mouth. She leaned into me as she reached up and closed the open window behind us.

Her hands gripped my shoulders as she fucked me the way I asked her to.

My hands clutched the bottom of her ass cheeks, spreading them wide as she bounced up and down. Each time I slid deeper into her and felt like I could have bust right then and there, but I held out.

I wanted to enjoy her longer.

She growled, pressing a hand on my chest and arching her back. She pushed her pelvis towards me and then started grinding to her own beat, whimpering every time she thrusted her hips forward.

"Let me get that nut," I coached her, reaching down to play with her clit. A slew of curse words left her mouth before her body started trembling against me, and all the blood rushed to my core. "Fuck, Yadah, you about to make this dick cum for you."

Her lips crashed into mine as I started thrusting my hips up at a rapid speed. Her fuck faces mixed with her titties bouncing in my face had me ready to risk it all.

"Fuck, Nelly," she moaned into my mouth. "Please cum for this pussy."

"Say it again," I commanded, and as soon as she did, I lifted her up just in time for my seeds to coat her stomach and not the inside of her walls.

"You good?" I asked, coming back into my cabin to find Yadah slipping on her top. After our session under the stars, we'd chilled for a little more before we had round two and three down here. It was now touching on four in the morning, and I was finally ready to knock the hell out.

"I'm great," she smiled my way. "I'm going to head to my room."

"Cool." When she got within reach, I gave her a hug and planted a kiss on the top of her left shoulder. "See you in a few hours. By the time we get back to the island, Deuce, Kristmas, and them should be there."

"Yup." She walked out of my room, only to reappear a moment later. "Hey, Nelly." She leaned up against the door frame, an unreadable expression on her face.

'"Sup?"

"You know how you said since we're both single and not tied to anyone really…"

"Mhmm," I responded, wondering where she was about to go with this.

"I was thinking," she fiddled with her fingers before giving me full eye contact, "…what if we have a little vacation fling?"

I crossed my arms over my bare chest as I suppressed my lustful smile. "So, you want me rearranging your guts this whole trip is what you're saying."

"Nelly," she sang through gritted teeth. Her flushed face made me smirk.

"That's what you're saying, though. Am I wrong?"

"All I'm saying, is that I wouldn't mind having some peen on demand for the entire trip with someone I know can deliver."

I smiled. "That's a fact. So, I'm wit' it." It was definitely an easy yes.

"Cocky."

"Confident," I corrected her. "And you the one who said I can deliver."

"Big mistake on my part," she joked. "Okay, cool. But there are some rules." I raised a brow. "For one, this has to stay between us. If anything, Kristmas definitely cannot find out."

"Oh, that's a definite." Kristmas was the last person I'd want to find out about me and Yadah. She loved me like I was biologically her baby brother, but she thought I was the ultimate hoe. There was no way she'd be okay with Yadah and me swapping bodily fluids, even if there were no feelings involved.

"The exception is if you need to tell Tiffani, you can. Long as you assure me no drama will come from it."

"I can tell you really don't believe how shit is with me and Tiff."

"It's a little shocking. I ain't gone lie."

"Me and Tiff have a 'if I want to know, I'll ask, and if I ask, I want to know. Otherwise, don't really feel the need to tell me something that really has nothing to do with me' kind of policy. So, I'm not about to go back to the hotel and be like, 'Yo, Tiff, I slept with Yadah'. But if she asked me about something, then yeah, I'll tell her, but either way, there won't be an issue."

"Okay, I won't bring it up again. Promise. And last rule, once we leave this island — that's it. This will not be an ongoing thing. This week and this week only. That way, there're no emotions, attachments, or expectations. Nothing more. Nothing less."

"Don't get hooked on the monster between your legs. Got it."

"Good, because once I get on that plane, your devil peen will be a figment of my imagination."

I cackled. "You sure that's all of your rules?"

"Yup. So, I'll see you later."

"Unless you want this devil dick to wake you up."

"See, that's how we will get caught," she said, shaking her head.

"Ain't nothing wrong with living on the edge, Kookie."

Her brows dipped in. "Kookie? What happened to Kooks?"

"I changed it. I like Kookie better."

"I'm not answering to that."

"You ain't gotta answer, but you better listen."

She rolled her eyes but couldn't hide the soft smile on her lips. "Good night, Nelly." She turned on her heels, and my dick couldn't help but jump as my eyes landed on her juicy bottom cheeks.

Yeah, I'ma enjoy sliding up in her all week. "Sweet dreams, Kookie."

Chapter 5
Yadah

"Hey, friend!" Kristmas sang as soon as she opened the door to their massive suite. It was one of the best suites in the hotel and was laid out like an apartment with a living room and kitchen, plus two bedrooms.

"Heyyy Krissy boo," I sang back, embracing her into a hug. "Is the food here? Because I'm already starving."

"Yes, girl," she said, pulling back and letting me into the suite. "And thank God you're here because THESE MEN are driving me crazy." She leaned in closer to whisper, "And Jay's girl is here, but per usual, she got that stank face on with her nose in the air."

I rolled my eyes. "He need to leave her ass home."

"That's what I said."

We shared a laugh as we headed deeper into the suite. Jonah — or Jay as most called him — was the middle brother of the Jacobs brothers clan. His girlfriend, Mariah, wasn't a fan favorite. I had only been around her once before, and her energy rubbed me wrong. However, Krissy had been around her enough, and if my best friend didn't vibe with someone, neither did I.

"I heard your ass talking shit about me and my boys. You wasn't whispering," Deuce said as soon as we got into his line of vision.

"I wasn't trying to whisper. I wanted you to hear me, with yo' big headed self," Krissy shot at him.

"Yo Yadah, you see how she talk to me and it's my birthday?"

"Boy, your birthday ain't until the weekend; stop fake whining," Krissy waved him off.

I shook my head and then laughed when Deuce snatched his wife to him. They were always the cutest, and every time I saw them, I was happy as hell my best friend gave him a second chance after he royally messed up in high school. But it just goes to show that time and maturity can truly heal certain wounds. Plus, Deuce showed he'd learned from his mistake.

My eyes glanced around the room, looking for Nelly. My yoni couldn't help itself. After we got back to the hotel the day before yesterday, I was full of excitement, thinking I was gonna be getting penis every night. However, I hadn't experienced the dangerous tool between his legs since the boat. Between everyone else arriving and Kristmas having our lives planned out to a T, we hadn't had time to link. My vagina was not happy about it. Not after I'd gone out on a limb and asked to have him on demand.

"I'm surprised Nelly ain't cook," I commented.

"I thought my ass was on vacation too. I cooked for y'all last night. That's all you getting." He emerged from the back, and the doors to orgasmic heaven seemed to open.

"Selfish," Jay commented from his spot on the couch.

"And?" Nelly retorted.

"Where is Tiffani and Dale?" I questioned, tuning out Jay and Nelly, realizing they were missing. Tiffani finally felt better yesterday and was able to come sightseeing with us. And just as Nelly had said, she was the same Tiffani I'd met on day one — talkative as hell, fun, and flirtatious.

"They went down to Tiff's room. She forgot to bring her passport," Krissy told me, causing a light bulb to go off in my head. Kristmas had reminded us three times last night that we'd need our passports for our adventures today, and I still forgot.

"Shoot, I forgot too." The sides of Krissy's mouth turned down. "You judging me and ion like that."

"Dale said he reminded you before he came up."

I poked out my mouth. "Dale be saying a lot in the morning, and I still be sleep. His ass be up at the crack of dawn, more hyper than a crackhead."

"Bitch, I heard that," Dale made his presence known.

"Am I lying?" I asked, peeking over my shoulder to see him flipping me off.

"Y'all two are a mess," Tiffani said. "Good morning, Yaya! Now we can eat!"

"Oh, y'all were waiting on me?" I grimaced and then smiled. "Whoops."

We devoured the breakfast and were sitting around, talking about some of everything when Nelly brought the attention to him. "So, I got a question."

"Yes, the food was better than yours," Jay said, taunting his little brother.

"Fuck you. Anyway, would y'all tell a woman that she hurt your feelings?" He looked at his brothers as Tiff and I kissed our teeth.

"Like on some punk ass shit?" Jay asked.

"Exactly on some punk ass shit," Nelly confirmed.

"I wanna say no, but y'all know X will blast my ass right in my face," Deuce stated his thoughts.

"And will," Krissy commented with a wide smile. "But ain't nothing wrong with that. I bet you think that makes you look weak, Nelly."

"Not think. Know. And we know Deuce weak as hell. He just lucky I let him get you."

"I will leave your ashes on this island and act like you never existed," Deuce warned his brother, and the entire table cackled. I was convinced Nelly loved getting his brothers riled up.

"It is a little weak sauce," Dale added.

"You hush," I slapped him on his arm. "Men should be able to express their feelings—especially Black men."

"For what reason? Y'all women will eventually throw it right back in our faces," Jay challenged, and I saw Mariah roll her eyes from beside him.

"You feel me, bro. I just don't see that shit turning into something healthy."

While Nelly continued to get everyone riled up, I snuck out to go get my passport and sneak in a few photos. We still had forty minutes to spare before our transportation arrived.

When knocks sounded on my door twenty minutes later, I was almost positive it was Kristmas on the other side. She texted me ten minutes ago, asking me where I was and to come save her from the Jacobs brothers' nonsense. However, it was definitely not her, and my yoni knew it.

Somersaults.

My vagina was an Olympian at the sight of Jonel Jacobs.

It was the fact that he could almost effortlessly make me cum, and that in itself was the ultimate turn on.

I almost didn't know how I'd not jump his bones after this week. However, if there was one thing I was, I was someone who wouldn't go back on my word.

"About time we get some alone time," he said, invading my space. The sound of the door closing was met with his lips on my shoulder, trailing up to my neck. His hands snaked their way inside of my kimono, down my back, and then underneath my behind before he lifted me up so that we were eye level. "What you up here doing?"

"I came to get my passport and to take a few pictures." I nodded to my tripod posted on the balcony. He carried me out there and placed me back on solid ground. We were on a high floor with a partial view of the ocean. I loved how private the balcony was with thick cement walls that went out further than the railing. In order to see our neighbors, we'd have to lean over the railing and snake out our heads as long as possible.

"You finna take my pictures for me?"

"No," he replied smoothly. His eyes demanded my attention as he watched my every move and ate my body up with just one look.

"So why you brought—"

"Turn around." I hesitated but then did as he requested. His hands rested on my shoulders, and I prayed that he couldn't see my body shiver at his touch. A soft kiss was placed on my shoulder before he removed my kimono and tossed it on one of the chairs near him. "Grab the railing."

I looked back at him, inquisitively, and his lust-filled eyes told me everything I needed to know. He was about to give my vagina everything she wanted right on this balcony. "Nelly, what if—" My words got caught in my throat when he started kissing up the side of my neck. His hands wrapped around my body and drew me closer into him before his fingers landed on the button of my coochie-cutting denim shorts.

"As soon as I seen you with your thighs all out, I knew I had to have you this morning," he whispered into my ear, and a puddle of my juices landed into the seat of my swimsuit.

I wanted to respond to that, but the only thing that managed to slip out of my mouth was a moan as he dipped two fingers into my soaking warmth. He massaged my clit at just the right speed before stopping just short of me creaming all over his palm.

"Why the hell you stop?" I snapped, and he smirked devilishly.

"You'll see." He pushed my shorts down my hips and over my ass before letting them drop to the ground. "Keep your hands on the railing," he commanded, spreading my legs apart.

I normally wasn't this passive when it came to sex. I was used to having to tell the men what I wanted from them, but Nelly took control, and it knocked me into a type of submission I didn't mind. At all.

It turned me all the way on instead.

I peeked over my shoulder to see him pulling the two chairs towards me. He placed one right next to me and the other behind me. "Put your leg up." He tapped my left thigh, and I placed my foot onto the chair, anxious for what would happen next.

He squeezed my exposed ass cheeks before tucking a finger into the seat of my swimsuit and pushing it to the side. His thumb caressed my swollen clit before I felt bliss.

"Fuck," I hissed seconds into his thick tongue devouring me from behind. "Oh, fuck."

"Mhmm," he hummed while making the best kind of slurping

sounds that made me know he wasn't leaving not even one little drop of my juices behind.

He ate me with straight conviction, and I respectfully came all over his face.

"Damn, you sweet and sticky like raw *kookie* dough."

I snickered. "I see what you did there." I went to put my foot down and pull the seat of my swimsuit back in its rightful place when he stopped me.

"Come on now, Kookie, don't play with me." My eyes landed on the golden wrapper he was now opening and then past that to his trophy dick print.

"Nelly, we probably got like ten minutes before we gotta head downstairs."

"Sounds like we got time then."

He pushed his bottoms down, and I shivered at the sight of my new friend, who was armed and ready to go to work. However, I knew that Krissy would kill us for being late and messing up her schedule.

Just as I was about to stand my ground, I faltered.

It was the shoulder kiss that completely made me come undone once more, and before long, he was slipping and sliding in me like my vagina was a water slide, inflated just for him on a hot summer day.

Holding my left leg up by the cuff of his arm, he drilled into me relentlessly, and I was more than positive that the rooms to the side and below us had to have heard the moans I tried so hard to suppress.

"SHIT!" I cried out, applying pressure to the railing as my juices trickled down my thigh from the orgasm that exploded through me. My knee wanted to give out on me, but I hadn't completed the task at hand.

"You got two minutes to make me cum for you," he growled into my ear. "So fuck me harder, Kookie."

I leaned into the railing and put added weight onto my right leg — *forget needing two good knees; one would suffice* — so I could throw my ass back the way he wanted me to. I threw it back in circles, matching his pace and being turned on even more each second by his rugged breathing.

"Fuck, like that," he grunted, tightening his grip on my waist. "You about to make me cum."

"That's what you want, right?" I said, gasping for my own breath because every time he tapped my cervix, I couldn't breathe.

"That's exactly what I want, and you about to get this shit."

"Give it to me," I coaxed him and almost regretted it as he went into overdrive, pounding the hell out of my coochie as if it robbed him until he released.

We were still catching our breath when I heard the door keypad beep. "Oh shit!" I blurted, scurrying out of Nelly's hold as another beep sounded. Thank God it always took Dale about three times before he got the room key to work.

I swiftly adjusted my swimsuit and pushed Nelly out of the door's line of vision mere seconds before it opened.

"See, I knew your ass was up here taking pics!" Dale chuckled, barely paying me any mind as he headed over to his side of the room. I kicked my shorts out of the way and pretended to check my phone as I stepped back into the room, hoping I didn't bring the stench of sex with me.

"You know me. I wanted to get a few in with this view."

"And with your peach on display! I ain't mad at you, boo. I almost forgot my damn flask." He held it up after grabbing it off of the night-stand. "And Krissy told me to tell you we heading down to the lobby in ten. You want me to wait for you?"

"No, no." I smiled, harder than necessary. "Go ahead and let them know I'm coming. I'm actually gonna change swimsuits real quick."

"You did bring more than enough."

"Hush up," I laughed, happy to see him heading towards the door.

"But bet! See you in ten!"

Dale was out of the room almost as quickly as he came, but my heart was almost out of my chest. As soon as the door closed, I whipped around, and my eyes landed on a fully dressed Nelly, who let off a round of laughs.

"I ain't think you had that much strength. Damn near knocked me through the wall."

I rolled my eyes. "You wasn't moving fast enough. He coulda been with Tiff or Krissy."

Nelly continued to laugh. "Calm down, Kooks. It's all good. This is what makes it fun."

He winked, gave me a kiss, and left me to freshen back up. Fun almost gave me a heart attack, but I'd do it again.

"CAN SOMEONE PLEASE REMIND ME WHOSE IDEA IT WAS TO WAKE UP AT the ass crack of dawn and hike up a volcano to see a sunrise I could see from my hotel room?" Krissy asked as we trekked up said volcano. We were on our second to last full day on the trip, and on today's itinerary was a sunrise hike. The hike up to the summit was expected to take almost two hours, which meant that we had to wake up at two-thirty this morning to get to the volcano and start the hike no later than four. Once at the top, we'd supposedly see one of the best sunrises ever. I'd seen a lot of pictures of it on social media, so unlike Krissy, I was actually excited to experience it. Plus, I enjoyed hiking.

"If I recall from the group chat, it was definitely Jay and Deuce."

"And look at they ass way in the back," Krissy said, and I laughed.

"We pacing ourselves!" Jay defended.

"Mhmm sure," Krissy said, "I shoulda been like your girl and opted out."

"Hell, me too," Dale commented from a few feet behind us. Me and Krissy were leading the pack as we followed our guide up the dark path. Behind us was Dale and Tiff, and behind them were the brothers.

The thought of Nelly potentially watching my ass by way of his flashlight sent tingles down my soul and straight up my vaginal canal. I couldn't wait to have him back between my thighs.

"How's married life this quarter?" I asked, trying to knock out the dirty thoughts of my mind and focus on something else.

"Better than the last," she cheesed, saying her standard answer that I knew to be true. My friend exuded happiness, and I loved it for her.

"I'm still waiting for you to pop up on one of my favorite ratchet shows."

She snickered. "Girl, Deuce would probably kill me if I told him I was about to be on Basketball Wives or some shit like that."

"The way they love his ass, I'm surprised he hasn't been offered his own show."

"Girl, same. They worship my baby. And speaking of babies," my eyes widened, and she quickly said, "I'm not pregnant! But," her smile widened. "We did decide that we're about to start trying. We're both ready for some little gremlins running us wild."

"Aww!" I sang, not able to contain my excitement. "I'm happy for y'all and can't wait for my godbabies."

"Keep this energy because if they come out looking like him, I'm shipping them away."

An hour later, we were watching the most awestricken sunrise I'd ever seen. Watching the sun rise through the clouds from this high above ground was something I didn't know I needed.

"So, you're still messing around with Marvin?" Krissy asked, and I inwardly rolled my eyes because this conversation could ruin my relaxed vibe. "Or have you moved on to dating single men? You know, ones who aren't attached to other women. Or men, if you're into that."

I let out a sigh. "Krissy, don't start." I couldn't fathom why she'd even started a conversation I knew she didn't want to have. Kristmas had made it perfectly clear years ago that she was not a fan of me being comfortable being a side chick. Yet, she stayed asking about my dating life, only to be disappointed when I told her that whoever my current contender was, was also in a relationship with someone else.

And so, I avoided talking to her about my situations because I wholeheartedly understood that most women wouldn't agree with how I lived my life — especially someone like Krissy, who dealt with Deuce cheating on her in high school with the school's biggest hoe.

"I just asked a question," she shrugged.

"One that you don't want the answer to because it's not gonna be one you like."

She huffed. "Kayadah." *Oh... she's full naming me. Here we go.* "I just don't get why you don't think you're worthy of a man who thinks you're more than just some ass when he wants a break from his wife. You're a whole package, and I just wish you'd see that."

"I do see that." And I did. I knew that my personality was uniquely me. I was smart, funny when I wanted to be, and had grown into a beautiful swan. But there was a lot of validation that came with being able to pull someone else's man, and that's what I needed.

"Do you?" She cocked her head at me. "In college, it was one thing, but now you're a whole grown ass woman who's never had her own man. And back then, at least it was just people's boyfriends. Marvin is someone's husband. And he's—"

"Okay Kristmas, damn. I don't need or want to be lectured. I already know your stance, and I get it. What I'm doing is fucked up, and you think less of me because of it, but this is my life. Let's just drop it. Please."

I looked around to make sure none of our people were within earshot.

"I'll drop it — for the remainder of this trip — after I say this." I rolled my eyes. "I might not like what you're doing, but you're my best friend. I'll never think less of you. I just know you can do better. You deserve better. And really, I just want you to be careful because it can end up being a dangerous situation, Ya."

"I always am. Besides, I'm probably going to end things when I get back." I fed her the same line I had Nelly because I needed it to be true. For the most part, I enjoyed what I had going on with Marvin. Yes, he wasn't fully mine, but up until recently, that hadn't mattered much.

But I was being sucked in by Marvin, and I knew that meant it was time for me to cut ties. I wasn't dumb. I never expected any man to leave their woman for me, nor did I ever ask them to. I played my role the way I told them I would, and when feelings got too deeply involved, I exited stage left.

I should have exited stage left at least three months ago. So, when I got back to Texas, I *needed* to end things with him.

That was why I welcomed Nelly as a distraction — carefree, bomb ass sex with someone I knew I wouldn't get wrapped up in. Nothing about Nelly and I made sense.

Besides his age and his very direct way of communicating, there was also my most recent addition to my invisible list —he made me feel out of control. I did not like that at all. I submitted to him with ease, and I wasn't the submissive type.

However, I was more than happy to be living out my fantasy of having him in between my legs and blessing me with mind-blowing sex. If only for this week.

"I'm gonna hold you to it," she said and then left me alone with my thoughts to go take pictures with her man and the view.

There were things about me I knew I needed to work on because sooner or later karma was going to bite my whole ass off.

"Follow my lead," Nelly whispered into my ear, making me jump. I snapped my head around just as he stood back upright.

"What?" I questioned to his back, but instead of answering me, he got all of our friends' attention instead.

"Who wanna race me back down?"

"Oh, hell no," Tiffani said from her spot beside Dale. Those two had really been attached at the hip. I might've been jealous if it wasn't for the fact that the more time they spent together, the more time Nelly got to play between my legs. "Are you serious? And all the way back down?"

"That fool definitely is," Jay spoke up, knowing his brother.

"I am, and nah, just down the steepest part."

"Oh no no no," Tiff sang.

"What happens when I win?" I said, standing to my feet and wiping the remnants of dirt off of my butt.

"You mean if y'all both don't die?" Krissy asked.

"My thoughts exactly," Dale commented.

"I would," Deuce sang, "but I just signed a new contract and—"

"Pussy," Nelly taunted. "Well, it looks like it's just me and you, X's friend."

Well played, Mr. Jacobs.

"Yadah, if you die, I'm not telling your mama so she can kill me."

I laughed at Krissy. "Who gon' send us off?" I asked as me and Nelly started towards the way down with our friends telling us to be careful.

"I'll send y'all off to your imminent death," Dale volunteered, making everyone laugh.

"You never answered what I get if I win," I eyed Nelly as we prepared to race.

"It's a surprise." He winked. I gagged.

Seconds later, Dale yelled, 'GO' and we took off .

This was definitely dangerous as hell, but I lived for adrenaline rushes.

We were more than halfway down the steepest part when I slipped and landed on my ass. "Oh shit," I gasped, causing Nelly to glance over his shoulder to see what had happened. He immediately double backed.

"You okay?" He extended a hand to help me up, and I yanked him right down beside me, knocking him off his square. I sprinted to my feet and took off.

"I'm fine!" I yelled, laughing.

I was still tittering to myself when he caught up to me at the *finish line*.

"You know you gonna have to pay for cheating."

"I didn't cheat. I really did bust my butt. It's not my fault I used it to my advantage. If you didn't want that to happen, you should have paused the race."

"A ha ha." He pulled me to him, doing that thing I hated but loved — planting a kiss on the top of my shoulder. He wrapped his arms around me. "You might like your punishment."

A smile spread across my face. "I know I will."

We continued to make our way down when I saw an opening off of the trail. "That looks like a little cave. Let's go check it out since we have time." I gripped his hand, guiding him the way I wanted.

"You're the type that likes to go off the beaten path."

"I've always been extra curious about the unknown. Besides, what's the worst that can happen?"

"We die, and I'm too cute to die at this young, ripe age."

We both had to duck as we navigated through the cave-like path. "We not gon' die. Maybe you will, but I'll live to tell the story."

Nelly chortled and smacked me on my ass as we emerged on the other side. The view was worth potentially dying for.

"Damn this is — everything." He took the words out of my mouth as we both took in the view of the island outline. Luminique was stunning.

"See. Aren't you happy you listened to me?"

"A lil' bit," he said, taking a seat on the edge of the cliff. This overlook was definitely not something for more than a few people at a time since there wasn't much space far from the opening of the cave to the edge of the cliff. I sat down next to him.

We were quiet as we both took in what nature had to offer us at this time of morning.

Nelly laid back on the ground and stared up at the picturesque sky that still had the colors of the sunrise lining it. "This is the kind of calmness I need sometimes to stop all the shit that be bouncing around in my head."

"Stuff about what?" I asked, eyeing him.

"Business, life, all that." He kept it short and then closed his eyes. My midnight brown orbs ran down his body until they landed on his penis.

I pushed myself back a little before leaning over and massaging the outline of his print. He didn't have to say anything for me to know his eyes were now on me. I licked my lips and pulled in my bottom lip before glancing his way.

The incredulous look on his face made me bite down on my lip harder. I tucked my hand into his workout shorts and pulled out my yoni's current best friend.

My mouth drooled at the sight of it, and I wanted it touching the back of my throat. Pulling a wet wipe from my fanny pack, I cleaned his penis before I swallowed him whole.

The moment he hissed in delight, I smiled and went to work.

My tongue swirled around the tip of his penis and sucked while my right hand moved up and down his shaft.

"Damn," he hummed.

My eyes met his as he adjusted his position so that he was resting on his elbows and able to enjoy the view — me sucking him off and the one behind me.

I ran my tongue down his length and back up before popping both of his balls into my mouth and gently tugging them.

His light moans turned me on, and I was determined to make him coat the back of my throat. I bobbed my head up and down with conviction once his dick was back in my mouth.

If I died, I died.

"Mhmm," I moaned as spit dripped down my chin and onto him.

"You gon' make me cum, Kookie?" His words were raspy as his eyes pierced through me. I didn't think giving someone head had ever turned me on this much.

I didn't answer him; I just finished what I had started and enjoyed every ounce of him.

Standing to my feet with a satisfied smirk, I rushed him. "Come on before our friends end up making it down before us."

"You gone have to carry me. You sucked all the energy out of me." Nelly grunted as he stood up and I cackled. "And just know, I don't care if we only make it back five minutes before them, I'm sliding into you in the back of the van."

"Negative. I'm all sweaty."

He pulled me to him for a kiss before we headed back through the cave-like pathway. "I said what I said."

I shook my head, laughing. "Nasty ass."

He smacked my ass, instructing me to lead the way. "You have no idea."

Chapter 6
Nelly

"So, Tiffani again, huh?" Deuce questioned. Me, him, and Jay were down at the hotel bar shooting the shit before they were to meet up with their significant others.

"And?" I responded. "She cool and everybody like her."

"Ain't nothing wrong with her, but this the second time, you brought her as your plus one."

"Third," Jay corrected. "Remember, he brought her to dad's fiftieth birthday party last year."

"I forgot about that," Deuce commented.

Here they asses go. "So, this what y'all do when you all wifed up? Keep tabs on me?" I motioned for the bartender to bring us another round. "Y'all fuckers pathetic. Focus on your women."

They shared a laugh. "You know we just messing with you, baby bro," Deuce said. "But it would be nice if you actually introduced us to someone you were actually dating."

"For y'all to embarrass me?"

"X is the one who would tell all your business," Deuce spoke facts.

"Exactly. Besides, even if I was dating someone seriously, I wouldn't bring her on a trip like this. That's how women get caught up, thinking marriage about to be next 'cause I introduced them to my family. Or that we more serious than we are." To avoid all that, I either came alone on any trips or brought Tiffani.

"I want to say that's bullshit," Jay said, "but I swear, after I started bringing Riah around y'all more, that's when she started hinting more at marriage and complaining about me spending so much time at the studio."

"See." I raised my drink before taking a sip. "But," I said, ready to stir the pot. "You and Riah have been together for a minute. What's holding you back?" My brothers, unlike me, had always been the relationship type, who wanted the *happily-ever-after-married-with-kids-and-a-picket-fence-dream*. And I loved that for them. So, despite how Mariah sometimes came across, I knew he loved the hell out of her.

"The pressure she's put on me to do it. I love her, and I'ma do it. I just want it to be on my terms. An ultimatum won't work, and she gotta remember that."

"Well, don't let that pride of yours cause you to lose her," I said and Deuce nodded his head in agreement.

"Yeah, I know. I just hate that she gets into these funky moods over things I can't control. She doesn't like this artist I'm working with, and we got into it right before the trip—"

"And that's why her nose been in the air all week," Deuce commented.

"I know those X's words," Jay said, and we all laughed.

"You know how your sister-in-law is. Thank God Yadah on this trip to keep her from speaking on it."

The mention of Yadah had the sides of my mouth curving up and the tip of my dick jumping. My mind veered back to her head bobbing up and down my length this morning. I had done some wild shit, but getting head while sitting on a cliff of a volcano was definitely something to remember.

"What time again in the morning?" The scraping of Deuce's bar stool pulled me back into the conversation.

"Pick up is at eleven-thirty. Don't let sis wear your ass out too much tonight," Jay answered him. We had some brotherly bonding time planned for his birthday. We were going on a local distillery tour and then ATVing around the island.

"I can't make any promises. She might get a baby out of me tonight." We cheered at that comment, and he left.

"You know he and X really starting to think you just a whole ass hoe instead of a half of one."

I sniggered and flipped Jay off. Since we lived in the same city, he had more insight to my dating life and knew a little bit more than Deuce about why I didn't care to bring women around.

"The way all my half-ass attempts at relationships have turned out, hoeing twenty-four-seven ain't looking too bad. I'll just live vicariously through y'all lovesick asses when I need to."

"Fuck you, bitch."

"That's what you got Mariah for."

"He is right about that." Mariah's voice caused us both to look over our shoulders. "Babe, you ready?"

"Yup." He stood as he finished his drink. "See you in the morning, baby bro."

"Back already?" Tiffani stated when I entered our room.

"Yup. My brothers got snatched up by their women, so I'm back to work your nerves." I grabbed a wine glass before joining her on the balcony. The view of the ocean took my breath away each time. "What we getting into tonight?" I grabbed the bottle of Chardonnay.

"Well *I* am going on a party bus tour with Dale and his boo since I thought you were gonna be busy with *yours*."

I paused my pour to meet her funky ass smirk. *She knew.* "What you know?" I asked with a chuckle.

"Everything," she sang before pushing at my shoulder. "And you know I'm ready to kick your ass because what happened to 'I don't want her'?" She mocked me, and I laughed. "She was supposed to be mine this week, and yet I get stuck with the dude who don't even like what I'm offering." I damn near spit out my wine at her extra ass.

"She was never gonna be yours. Let's not forget about all that lost cause flirting you were doing."

She flipped me off, laughing. "You not shit for bringing up the past. That doesn't negate my point. I *thought* you didn't want her."

"I didn't." *Then.* But now, I wanted my tongue buried inside of her sweetness. "But if I recall I also said, if she was offering up her pussy on a platter, I would fuck. So here we are."

"Hmmm," she hummed. "I guess you have me to thank for that. Dale and I both agree y'all are cute together."

"Dale?"

She sipped her drink. "After he found out how me and you roll, he told me he thought he heard y'all having sex on that boat but wasn't sure." I snorted. So much for us trying to be quiet. "And from there, we became FBI agents and started noticing y'all subtle interactions and how y'all kept disappearing around the same time. I bet y'all did something nasty on that mountain this morning, 'Mr. Who Wanna Race'."

I cackled at that. "So, you ain't missing daddy's dick?"

"This might come as a shock, but I don't come on these trips to fuck you. I come for the free trip."

"Fuck you," I said, laughing.

She giggled. "I mean, you're an added bonus, but I already have access to you whenever I want. Let my boo enjoy you. Besides, it's actually been one of the highlights of me and Dale's trip, watching y'all secret romance unfold."

"Romance?" I scoffed.

"Yup. You must have forgot, I watched y'all have sex for the first time, and that shit was fire. Y'all just have some kind of chemistry that's not hard to see."

"Yeah, sexual chemistry. That's it."

Tiff balled up her face. "No, what *we* have is sexual chemistry. What y'all have is more than that. *You* don't want to see it."

"Or maybe you need to get your eyes checked." I shrugged.

"How about this, if something more ever comes from this, you owe me five hundred dollars."

Kookie Dough

I chortled as knocks sounded on the door, and she grabbed her purse. "That's money you'll never see."

"Never say never," she said, giving me a quick kiss. "And let Yadah know I don't mind sharing *her* with you."

I shook my head, laughing, as she left.

Chapter 7
Yadah

I stared down at the passive aggressive text I'd just sent Marvin, and after counting to five, I deleted it from the chat before he could see it. Earlier that day, I'd sent him a spicy video of me in a swimsuit, dancing, and he had yet to acknowledge it. The fact that it bothered me was a huge red flag for me. Deeper feelings were rearing its ugly head and I needed to nip it in the bud immediately.

Sighing deeply, I went through my hygiene bag, looking for my ibuprofen. I felt an annoyance headache coming on.

When I saw my box of tampons, I silently thanked Mother Nature for being nice to me by not making an appearance on this trip and ruining my sex fun with Nelly.

Freaking Jonel.

I couldn't suppress the flush of desire that rushed through me at the thought of him. And my yoni tingled, thinking about every last one of our encounters, even down to the quickest one.

He'd kept his word this morning, and when we got back to the van, he sexed me — sweaty vagina and all. We were very close to getting caught, but God must have been on our side—again.

"I don't know how you're not exhausted," I said to Dale as I emerged from the bathroom. He was putting on the final touches to his outfit.

"'Cause I'm not old like you."

I rolled my eyes but didn't disagree. The trip was starting to weigh me down. At twenty-seven, I couldn't hang like I used to, and it was showing. "Shut up. I'll be recharged and ready the turn the hell up tomorrow night."

"Heaux, I would hope so."

Tomorrow was Deuce's birthday and our last night on the island. Krissy had a turn-up event planned to celebrate her hubby right.

Dale and I talked some more before he left me to cuddle up with some Netflix and room service. Everyone else had been smart to take a nap when we got back from hiking. My ass decided to explore more, and now, my bed was all I needed.

I was thinking of another passive aggressive text to concoct when my phone dinged in my hand, and Nelly's name popped up.

My yoni's imaginary head poked out to read the text too.

NELLY

Busy?

The simple question sent something stirring in my tummy. I thought he'd be hanging out with Tiffani tonight. As far as I knew, everyone was coupled up tonight. Dale was going partying with Ackley. Krissy told me she was making sure Deuce brought in his birthday in the best way. *Freaks.* And I figured that Jay was going to be at Mariah's beck and call.

That left Nelly to spend time with the person he'd come here with. And me exactly where I was — loving on some tacos.

ME

Netflixin… wanna join? ••

I'll bring the chill 🍸

"They know," Nelly said as soon as I opened the door for him ten minutes later.

My eyes bulged as I grabbed his elbow and dragged him inside. He snickered as I said, "Who knows? Please don't say your brothers." My hands covered my face as I groaned.

"Nah. Dale and Tiffani."

"Of-fucking-course." He gave me a rundown of what Tiffani had told him, and all I could do was shake my head. I don't know why I thought we'd get away with hiding it from my *secret agent* ass friend. Dale rarely missed anything.

It made a whole lot more sense why he hadn't been jumping down my throat about hanging out with him and had been attached to Tiffani and Ackley's hip. Dale was a lot of things, but a *dickblocker* wasn't one.

I let out another deep sigh. "Long as Krissy and your brothers don't know, I can live with it." I climbed back on my bed with him following. "Oh! Are you hungry? I ordered pizza and tacos like a fat ass and haven't touched the pizza."

"Say less." He clapped and rubbed his palms together before heading over to where the spread of delicious food set.

"You gotta be cheating!" Nelly said, almost two hours later.

Time was flying by, and we'd surprisingly spent the time playing phone games and having random ass conversations about nothing. We were currently playing a trivia game, and Nelly was being a sore loser.

"Or you just need to stick to cooking 'cause you're just not that smart. Thank God yo' daddy helped you in the looks department, too."

The pillow from behind him came flying right into my face.

"Jonel!" I screeched, flailing my arms as I lost my balance and fell off of the bed.

Nelly's laugh might have woken up the entire floor, but I was ready to fight him.

"My bad, Kooks. I saw that going differently." His snicker made me flick him off before he helped me up.

"Get out." I pointed at the door.

"Damn, before I get some of that *Kookie dough* you're keeping warm for me?"

He ran a hand up my thigh, and I slapped it away. "No more cookies for you on this trip." *Yeah right.*

His brows rose. "It's cute how you lie to yourself."

"Hush." I shot him the bird again before I royally beat him the rest of the game.

"You must secretly be a dork. Some of those questions were random as hell."

I shrugged. "I like knowing random things." Knowledge really was power. "So," I sang, refilling both of our glasses with alcohol. "I got a question."

"Shoot."

I handed him his glass before climbing back in the bed. "Is Mariah as anti-social and standoffish as she seems? 'Cause you know Krissy got me side-eyeing her." That question had been at the forefront of my brain ever since we went sightseeing. Now was my chance to be nosey and get someone's opinion other than my best friend.

Nelly snorted. "X ain't shit. But Riah cool in small settings from what I've witnessed. When I hang out with them in Southgate, she not that bad. I like her most times. But when she get in her bag over something she doesn't like, she don't hide it well."

"Yeah, I can tell she and Jay ain't on the best of terms this trip."

"Hit the nail on the head. He told me and Deuce earlier that they got into it before they left. Not to mention, she's been pressuring him to marry her. So being around Deuce and X sappy asses probably ain't helping."

I grimaced. Another reason why I preferred my men already attached. I wouldn't get caught up thinking or wanting more. I knew better.

Reminder to self. End things ASAP with Marvin so you don't end up looking stupid.

"Women gotta stop thinking that pressuring a man is the way to go," he continued. "That's why that whole marriage shit ain't for me."

"Really?" My brows knitted themselves together. Nelly had the reputation of being the *most* hoeish one of the Jacobs brothers, but I still assumed he'd one day settle down with someone. "I always thought how you admired Deuce and Krissy's relationship meant you'd want that too."

"You can admire something that someone has and not want it." I nodded at the truth in that statement. "I love what my brothers have found with the women they're with, but they've both always been the relationship type. Even with Deuce and his big ass hoe phase. I thought it was cool, too, but after my mom passed, I realized a lot of the shit I wanted was because of her.

"The whole kids and family thing. I wanted to give her grandbabies who she could spoil like me, but…" he paused, and I noticed how hard it still was for him to talk about his mom, who passed almost three years ago. "Anyway," he shook his head, "none of that is me. I don't want the whole picket fence family shit. Not to mention, kids and me don't really agree."

"You're still young; that could change."

He snorted. "I doubt it. The only thing I care about is cooking and fucking. Those are the things that make me happy." He winked, and I shook my head. "I was having a similar conversation with my brothers about this when they commented on my bringing Tiff again. Them niggas want me to be whipped like they asses so bad."

I giggled. "You not right."

"I'm not lying either."

"You've really never brought someone you were dating to a family function besides Tiff?"

"Nah, my family is a big deal to me. So, they'd have to jump through plenty of fucking hoops before I'd even consider inviting them to anything family or close friends related. Tiff is the exception because we're one in the same when it comes to relationships and sex. And she cool as fuck, so I know she won't trip or embarrass me in front of my family."

"I guess that means you've never been in a serious relationship?" A question I found comical to ask someone else.

"Never with someone who actually 'brought something to the table'." I made a face at his air quotes. "And by that, I mean they always seem to want more from me than what they are offering or can do for themselves." He shifted his weight. "I'm together. All my shit is together, and they're wanting all of *this* from me. They see me and they see business is going good and who I'm connected to.

"But they're lacking ambition, or they don't have any follow through. They have all these dreams, but they're not working towards them. And then they don't wanna be *domestic* either. It's like pick a struggle, shorty, because you're expecting me to marry you or wanting me to have a baby with you. And I'm just like, 'yo, you're barely good enough for me to hang out with, let alone actually take you serious if you ain't got nothing really going on for yourself. And really, you just looking for a sponsor, and it ain't gone be me'."

"Life of a pretty boy who can cook." And got a trophy dick.

He chortled. "I guess, but I've also dealt with women who try to use me to get to Deuce." He shook his head. "That shit is tired because I'll be damned if I ever let some hoe ruin what he has with X."

"Yeah, 'cause Krissy will kill him this time, and I will help her bury him."

"Shit," he sang. "Count me in as well."

We shared a laugh.

"But seriously," he said as he searched for a movie. "I'd rather keep things with women casual 'cause I don't really have time for the bull-shit. I'ma tell them what I'm looking for or the type of energy I'm willing to put in, and they either yay it or nay it. If I start feeling like they expecting too much or can't handle casual, I ghost they ass."

"Jonel!"

He laughed and dodged my slap to his bicep. "What?"

"That's immature."

"Well, we can't all be a grown up like you, Kookie." A shiver of *fuck me* shot through my coochie. The name had grown on me — especially the way he tended to say it, as if he knew he could control me with it — and I hated it.

He placed a kiss on the top of my shoulder, draped an arm around me, and pulled me into his side to cuddle just as he pressed play on the movie.

There was no chill. Just Netflix.

And barely any of that for me.

I don't think I made it through a third of the movie. I woke up this morning with drool on my chin, my head rested on his chest, and my leg draped over his. A complete feeling of peace danced within me as my eyes adjusted around us.

Dale's leg hanging off the side of his bed came into view. *Damn.*

I had been so deep in my slumber that I hadn't heard him come in. If he didn't know before about me and Nelly, he'd know now.

"Hey," I said, gently coaxing Nelly awake. He made a soft humming noise in response. "It's after ten."

"Shit," he groaned. "I need to go." He and his brothers had some brother bonding thing happening to celebrate Deuce turning a ripe twenty-eight.

It was another five minutes before we both untangled ourselves from the other.

"I see someone enjoyed my warmth," he said, and I frowned. "I'm just saying, with all that crust around your eyes—"

I gasped and immediately pushed him forward and damn near into the door. I peeked at myself in the entry way mirror and inwardly groaned. There, indeed, was my eye crust being disrespectful as hell. "You're an ass."

"You like it, Kookie, don't act like you don't." He pulled my attention back to him.

"I tolerate it for the greater good." I eyed his penis, and he chuckled before opening the room door. He paused in the archway, and my eyes slowly dragged up his tall frame. *Why on earth was he this fine?* The Jacobs men really had an unfair advantage over most. They got it honestly, though. Their dad was also still as fine as aged wine.

We both stared awkwardly at one another.

I didn't know what to say. Last night felt *different.*

It was like our night on the boat before sex was back on the table.

Just real, raw, authentic conversation.

But this time, sex *was* on the table, and we both just chose to enjoy the other's company instead.

"Th—"

"I'll—"

We both spoke at the same time, stopped, then chuckled awkwardly.

"I was just gonna say, thanks for letting me vent or whatever it was I was doing last night," he said, with a small smile. "I didn't know I needed it."

The sides of my mouth curled up. "Glad it was good."

He winked and tapped the door. "Anyway, I'll see you later, Kooks."

"See you." I closed the door with my bottom lip pulled into my mouth and a stirring in the pit of my stomach. *No. Nope. Nah. Kayadah, hell n—*

"How's the dick?" Dale's voice made me jump out of my skin.

I was still holding my hand up to my chest when I said, "How long you been waiting to ask that?"

"Too fucking long," he turned over and stretched, "now tell me everything."

I plopped back down on my bed. "What's left to tell that you and Tiff haven't already figured out?"

"For one, how did you snag the D?! I, for one, am shocked because though he's fine as all hell, I've always known you to date more *mature* men. You know — old."

"I didn't need clarification." I rolled my eyes. But he was right. The last time I dated someone even my age was college. I didn't do youngins. But this was just dick.

"Was it our island-hopping adventure? 'Cause that's when I caught on. I thought I had dreamed it 'cause y'all was anything but quiet." My mouth dropped open. "It's a boat, boo, and you was rockin' it like Aaliyah."

I let out a laugh. "I really hate you."

"So back to my original question. How's the dick?"

I fanned myself. "You ever went to Chick-Fil-A and there was no line? It feels that good." Dale jumped out of his bed and started doing a praise dance. "OR you ever had to pee so freaking bad that you almost pissed yourself? And then when you get to the bathroom and you let it out? It just feels like fucking heaven, and you be thanking God. It feels like that."

"Oooh, you're in danger, girl."

"Trust me, I would be if I was young and dumb, but I know to take this exactly for what it is AND we both know Jonel is not the kind of man for me."

"But with a dick like that, exceptions shou—"

"Shut up, Dale!" I tossed a pillow at him and headed towards the bathroom to get my morning hygiene together.

"Just saying."

I went inside the bathroom and decided to rip the Band-Aid off. There was one thing Dale clearly did not know.

"And Dale," he looked over at my head sticking out of the door, "… it actually started with a threesome. You might wanna ask Tiff how this is all *her* doing." With that, I closed the bathroom door while laughing at him yelling, "Bitch, come again?!"

Chapter 8
Nelly

"Somebody's in here," I quipped at the person banging on the bathroom door.

"Fuck," they whined, "I gotta pee!" *Well, they better hope that the people in one of the other two ain't fucking as well.*

I pulled my lip in as my eyes sucked in Yadah's ass cheeks clapping back on my dick as I slid in and out of her. The sight of her creaming on the condom and the one of us fucking in the mirror were in competition. I wanted to look at them both at the same time.

"Mmm shit, Nelly," she crooned. "Just like that!" I looked into the mirror to see her squeezing her eyes closed and holding onto the edge of the counter while her titties almost broke free from the one shoulder crop top she had on.

Watching her take all of me and loving it added a new level to this session.

My right hand wrapped around the front of her throat and pulled her into my chest. Her pussy juices dripped down the inside of my thigh as I used my left hand to finger her.

"Look at yourself when you about to cum for me."

I moved my dick slowly in and out of her, torturing myself in the process while massaging her G-spot. Her eyes focused on me through the mirror. I applied pressure on her clit while quickening my pace.

"Shit," she hissed, bucking against me and shutting her eyes back closed.

"Open them," I commanded. "I want you to see how fucking gorgeous you look cumming on this dick."

"Fuck, I can't!"

"You fucking better," I gritted, barely able to get it out as my own nut came to a head.

My movements became erratic as her convulsions started.

Her mouth dropped open.

Our eyes locked.

And we finished together.

"WELL, THAT WAS ONE WAY TO WRAP THIS UP," YADAH SAID, REAPPLYING her lipstick. We had both finally pulled ourselves back together and was getting ready to head back out to the party.

Deuce's birthday celebration at a local rooftop club that overlooked the ocean was in full effect. We were in the VIP section, which thankfully came with its own set of bathrooms that Yadah and I had taken advantage of.

Our friends were busy drinking and partying, and we were in the restroom fucking.

"What you mean wrap it up? You should know that I plan to get me one more spoonful of your *Kookie dough* before we get on those planes tomorrow."

She rolled her eyes at me through the mirror, and I kissed the top of her bare shoulder. The two piece, all red outfit she had on was mesmerizing against her dark skin. And the thigh- high split of the skirt is what had me sneak a rub on her booty earlier, only for me to find out she ain't have on no draws.

I knew then she wanted me to fuck her in this bathroom.

"We have all of fifteen hours before we need to be at the airport. Exactly when do you expect to get in another session?"

"I was planning on going for one last sunrise beach run in the morning. I can change that to a sunrise Kookie fest instead." I licked my lips as she cackled, catching my drift. "One last *meal* with a view is what I'm thinking."

I gave myself one final look over as she fixed her hair. "What do you say, Kookie?"

"I'll think about it."

"I heard yes. See you back out there." I kissed her on the cheek and then unlocked the door.

I opened the door, and Yadah gripped my elbow, bringing my attention back to her. "Text me what time I need to be up once we get back to the hotel."

The sides of my mouth turned up as I squeezed a handful of her ass as I agreed to her request.

She went back to busying herself with her hair, and I stepped out of the restroom. My eyes met my oldest brother, and I quickly closed the door. But from the way his eyes fixed in on me — *on us* — I knew it was too late.

Shit.

He continued to another restroom, and I went back to partying it up in his honor.

"Yo, can I get a water?" Deuce said, coming up beside me at the bar an hour later.

"Water? What kind of birthday behavior is that?"

"Apparently not the kind you be on." The shade in his statement couldn't be missed. I knew he wouldn't drop what he saw. I was just happy that Yadah hadn't peeped him *peeping* us.

"It's nothing," I said, ready to get the conversation over.

"I wasn't about to say nothing."

"Yeah the fuck right. Just," I turned to him, "don't tell your wife."

"I'm drunk, not dumb. Kristmas would ring both of our necks if she found out you out here smashing Yadah, let alone doing it while Tiffani in the same vicinity."

"I promise you, it's not that deep, and you know Tiff and I situation. She don't care who or what I do."

"Yeah, but X won't see it that way. Yadah is her family." The bartender set his water in front of him.

"I know that, which is why none of y'all were supposed to find out."

"How long has it been going on?"

"Just this week," I admitted. "And only this week."

"Does Yadah know that?"

"It was *her* idea." He raised a brow because he probably saw Yadah the way I did prior to experiencing her undercover freak side. "Just sex while we're here. No strings or bullshit. So, like I *said*, it's nothing."

"Aight," he said, wrapping a hand around his water and stepping back from the bar, "but if this shit ever blows up in y'all face — ion know shit! Motherfuckin' Ray Charles!"

"Pussy," I yelled at his back with a chuckle.

Chapter 9
Yadah

"Stop pouting," I said to Krissy as we wrapped each other in a hug. "We're gonna see each other in three weeks!" The official countdown to my birthday had begun, and Kristmas was coming to visit me in Texas.

"I know, but still. I always miss spending time with you, boo. My Cali friends are cool but—"

"They not me. Won't ever be me. I get it."

"You can be so cocky at times," she said, laughing.

"I know, right."

"Now go before you miss your flight." We were standing outside of the security area of the airport. Dale, Tiffani, Nelly, Jay, and Mariah had already gone through. Deuce and Krissy were flying private and heading to one more island to finish off his birthday trip with a bang.

For my sis's sake, I hoped literally and figuratively.

Kristmas insisted on walking me as far as possible within the airport for our final goodbyes. Sometimes we were dramatic for no reason.

"Okay, okay. Have fun in Aruba," I said. "And make sure you come to Texas with my niece or nephew in your belly."

"Girl," she chuckled, "we just started trying. At least let me get in one last hot girl summer memory with you next month."

I rolled my eyes. "If you must." We hugged again, and then she waited until we couldn't see each other anymore once I went through security.

After I found my gate, I dropped my carryon luggage off with Dale and went to go find the restroom. I couldn't believe this trip was actually done, and I, of course, was not ready to get back to my regular life.

I relived my bladder then stood in front of the mirror, contemplating if I wanted to message Nelly. I didn't know the exact time of his flight, but I assumed he was still here since we'd all booked return flights around the same time. We hadn't said much to one another all day since every last one of us was recovering from last night's festivities.

The plans me and Nelly made last night, after he had me lose every ounce of my sanity while I watched him sex me in the restroom mirror, didn't go as planned. We'd ended up partying to the wee hours of the morning, and all any of us wanted to do was sleep for the few hours we could before we had to check out.

My hand hovered over the send button, but I chickened out.

The trip was over and so should our messages to one another.

I headed back through the terminal with my stomach growling. As I approached my gate, my eyes found Dale right where I'd left him, engulfed in his phone. I pulled out my phone to send him a text and made a one-eighty.

"Shit," I yelped, bumping right into someone. "Sor—Jonel!" I shrieked once my eyes landed on his sexy ass face. He smirked down at me. "Why are you sneaking up behind me?"

He chortled. "I wasn't. I was coming from the men's room and saw you."

"And followed me," I said, walking around him and heading towards the pretzel shop I'd passed. I texted Dale to ask if he wanted something.

"Damn. I guess a nigga can't even come give you a proper goodbye."

I forced back my smile.

"Well, aren't you the gentleman?"

"Jana and Jonathan might've taught me some kind of act right," he said, referring to his parents. "What time do y'all board?"

I glanced at my phone. "In about forty minutes, you?"

"A little less. Come with me right quick." He placed my hand in his, and it made my body do that dumb thing she did whenever he touched me. *Spazz.*

"Come with you where?" I put some resistance in my footing, but really, there was none. My yoni was now in pique curiosity.

"You'll see." He glanced back at me but didn't stop leading the way. Shortly thereafter, he was pushing us into a catty corner on the other side of the terminal next to an emergency exit door and a ninety percent empty gate.

"Nelly, what are you—" I gasped and slapped his hand away when I felt it pulling the band of my biker shorts away from my skin. "Airport! Lots of people walking by. Are you serious right now?"

The lust in his eyes told me the answer to that.

"Anyone can see us!" I said, since he was just staring at me, and I was getting wetter by the second.

"If you put your arms around my neck, it'll just look like we over here making out."

My heart was racing.

His six-foot something frame was towering over my five-foot-six one, but I could still see to the side of him. I could *see* people walking by. None of which looked our way, but still.

"Come on, Kookie, all I want to do is make you cum all over my hand, so I can lick it off and then have your juices marinating my tongue my whole flight."

I might've cum from that sentence.

My deep brown cheeks had to be showing red.

The rush that I was getting just from the *thought* of him making me cum in this airport surrounded by people made me think about how he'd pushed me well outside of my sex comfort zone all week.

I never thought my sex life was boring until now.

I had good sex.

But the sex I'd had this week had to be the type that made women ride by a man's house and check to see if the hood of his car was cold to make sure the peen didn't go anywhere. And of course, be a whole neighborhood watch to make sure no one came to said peen.

He had devil dick energy, which meant that it didn't matter if it was his penis, his fingers, or his tongue — you were fucked.

I was fucked.

And that was exactly why my arms wrapped around his neck like he instructed.

His thumb rubbed my clit while he seemed to be strumming my pussy lips like his very own personal instrument.

He placed his forehead against mine as my breathing became labored.

My eyes darted around because I just *knew* we were gonna get caught.

If not by Airport security, by some person recording us for social media clout.

"Close your eyes, Kookie," Nelly instructed as if he were reading my thoughts.

I did just as he slipped a finger into my opening. I hissed and then chomped down on my lip to keep my mouth closed.

"Just as warm and wet as I knew you'd be," he whispered.

Pressure built in my gut.

"You should really get a piercing here," he said, moving his thumb in circles over my clit hood. "So next time, I can have more to play with."

My eyes opened at *next time.* "There's no next time. This is —" *Find your breath, girl.* "It. Those were the—fuck." My hands applied pressure to the back of his neck. "Rules," I said after a second. "Those were the rules."

I could barely speak as the feeling of bliss continued to raise through my core.

Nelly smirked. I hated when he did that as he controlled my body. "You right. But if you change your mind—"

"I won't." He switched up the rhythm of his fingers, giving me a slight break from combusting. "Besides, isn't that what you like? Women who mean what they say when it comes to what they want from you? If this becomes a recurring thing, it will blow up in one of our faces. It's better as a one and done."

He slipped two fingers back into me and moved them in a come hither motion, instantly taking me back to the edge.

"Well then, I guess you're just gonna have to cum hard as fuck for me one last time." It was the way he said *cum for him,* mixed with the pressure of his thumb on my clit, and the rhythm of his fingers, that completely did it for me.

My eyes squeezed back shut as my body transported into oblivion.

Just as I was about to say fuck this airport and scream out loud, Nelly's lips covered mine, and I growled into them as I came all over his hands in a way that had me embarrassed to look at him once he inched his hand from between my legs.

I slowly opened my eyes and immediately looked around before getting turned on by him, licking my cream off of his fingers.

How could he so easily make me want to throw every bit of sanity I had out of the window and just have sex with him in the middle of this airport for all to watch?

I pulled a wet wipe from my stash in my fanny pack and handed it to him.

"Can we go find a restroom? We need to start heading back, and I still gotta get my pretzel."

He nodded and led the way.

After I did as good of a hoe bath as possible with my wipes, I met Nelly back out front, and we headed to the pretzel shop.

"Now that we're friends," he said as we stood in line.

"Oh, we're friends now?" I joked.

"Unless you wanna go back to being *X's friend,* but I did slide up in you more than three times; I think that constitutes more than acquaintances."

I chuckled. "You got a point."

"So now that we're friends, you gotta promise me something." I glanced at him with a raised brow. "Promise me that you won't be out here just giving your specialty *kookie dough* out to just anybody."

I looked away from him, wondering if he was about to be Kristmas number two. *Him* of all people.

"Like I told you on the boat, I ain't judging you on what you do, Yadah. But after getting to know you a bit more this week, beyond the sex, you really do deserve to be someone's wife. You're fun, adventurous, sexy as hell, and you got some superior ass pussy— you shouldn't be out here settling."

"Maybe I don't want to be somebody's wife. It's okay for you to not want to be somebody's husband. It's the same thing."

He looked at me unapologetically as he stated, "*You* want to be somebody's wife."

"Maybe I just want to be wanted."

"And that's not good enough. Not for somebody like you."

His words floated around in my head as we ordered our pretzels. I knew like Krissy, he was only looking out for me, so I tried my best to take his words for what he meant them to be.

"My bad if it wasn't my place to say that," he apologized as we waited for our food. "But you know me."

"It's all good. I'll take all you said into consideration, Mr. Jacobs."

And I would. I found it annoyingly cute that he seemed to care.

We received our pretzels and stepped back in the pathway of the slew of people. "I'm this way," Nelly pointed in the direction we'd come from. "Tiff just texted that we're boarding."

"Okay." I paused before saying, "Well, I'll see you around, Nelly."

"See you later, Kookie." He pulled me into a hug and planted a kiss on my left shoulder. The shoulder that I'd now deemed my favorite. "Now walk away, so I can watch that ass one more time."

I rolled my eyes and shook my head. "Bye, Jonel!" I pushed him away, and he laughed. "Do not watch me."

"I'ma watch." He licked his lips, and my yoni screamed, *don't leave him; kidnap him!*

Reluctantly spinning on my heels, I started towards my gate, refusing to look back to see if he had those mesmerizing eyes on me. I didn't have to look; I felt them.

"Hey, Kookie," he called, causing me to turn around to see a grin on his face. "So, tell me, how well did my young ass handle *it?*"

My mouth immediately spread into a grin that matched his. He had definitely made me eat my words of him not being able to handle my grown woman coochie.

I walked back into his space because my body needed one last moment of living in the fantasy we never expected to come true. And one last kiss, too.

"You handled it well and graduated with honors." My lips met his, and I loved that I could still taste myself on his tongue. I hope he savored it, like I planned to savor this memory of us. "Definitely vale*dick*torian."

The End and...

...The Beginning (again)
Weeks, Months, Years Later

"**Y**o Chef," one of my sous chefs, Marty, said, poking his head into my office. "There's a woman out here saying she got an interview or something with you right now."

"Shit," I said, looking up from what I was doing. "Send her back."

"Aye, what position you bringing her on for? I can tell she like to eat; my kind of woman."

I shook my head. Marty was a fool. "Nah. Leave this one alone 'cause you the reason I'm hiring another assistant now since—"

"Alright, I'ma head out." He shot me the deuces and disappeared, knowing the bullshit I was about to taunt him with. I let off a round of laughs at his expense. The truth was, my second-to-last assistant was so up Marty's ass, she was now his expecting baby mama. And Marty wasn't too happy about that.

While I waited for my two o'clock, I checked my group chat with my brothers, which was blowing up. "Oh shit," I said to myself as I saw the picture Jonah had sent to us of the engagement ring he'd gotten. He was *finally* about to do this shit, and all it took was for them to break up. Love was wild.

A throat cleared and I smiled, looking up into the face of the deep, umber-skinned beauty I hadn't seen in over two years.

There stood Kayadah Kookman, still gorgeous as ever and thicker than before. The knee length pencil skirt she had on hugged her hips like it had been designed for her. I couldn't help but imagine her thighs squeezing together to keep that *kookie* she housed between her legs warm and cozy.

My dick jumped.

"Kookie." A smile covered her face, but didn't reach her eyes. "How you been?" After our vacation fling, we became friends on social media, but a couple of months after, her accounts disappeared, and she seemed to as well. She hadn't attended any of the trips X had planned since, and I had almost started to wonder if it had anything to do with me — until a few weeks ago when X reached out to me and asked if I was still in need of a personal assistant.

Apparently, Yadah had moved back to Southgate three months ago and was having a hard time finding a job. And I was having a hard time keeping an assistant. I needed someone who could keep both my personal and professional life together for me because for the last year, I'd been failing at it. However, the last three assistants I'd had didn't seem to understand what I needed from them. I ended up feeling more overwhelmed, burnt out, and stressed.

"Good. You?"

"Good, but I'm hoping that will turn to great now that you're here." I sat on the edge of my desk. There was that half-ass smile of hers. Something about her energy and demeanor wasn't the Yadah I was used to, even prior to me exploring every ounce of her body — inside and out. She was reserved, timid, and acting like we barely knew each other.

"Well, thanks for meeting with me." Her hands squeezed the folder she held in her hand. "Would you like to see my resume? I know I may seem a little overqualified for the job but—" I let off a snort at her spill. "What?"

"I don't know why you're acting all professional. I don't care what your resume says. If you can do the job and you want it, it's yours. Name your rate."

"Oh. I thought this was gonna be an interview."

"Come on, Kooks." I stood, stuffing my hands into my pants

pocket. "X told me you needed a job and could do it without question, so that was all I needed to hear. I told her to tell you to come in so we could get the necessary paperwork done. And seeing you wouldn't hurt."

"Nelly."

Her apprehensive tone made me clarify. "What? You basically dropped off the face of the earth. So, it's good to see you, Kookie."

This time, her smile was genuine. "You too, Jonel."

"Just know this, I don't play when it comes to business and getting shit done. I need you to make sure that I get shit done, that I'm where I'm supposed to be. Make sure I'm not overbooked and that I make time for things that keep me balanced and not burnt out. My last few assistants couldn't keep up with what I needed from them. I need someone who will basically keep track of my day to day, whether it's business related or just life. Can you do that?"

"Tell you what to do and when to do it, absolutely."

"Great." I clapped my hands together. "Let's get the paperwork completed, and then how about we grab some food and catch up?"

"Nelly, look, I appreciate the job, but I really want to keep this professional."

Picking up on what she was insinuating, I said, "Yadah, you do know I know how to eat and not just *eat*." I lowered my eyes to what laid between her legs.

"Nelly, I'm serious. I really *need* this job." The hint of desperation in her voice caused a slight alarm to go off in my head, but I ignored it.

"And *I* need someone who can do the job. So, I hear you. Would you like to put new rules in place?" I was being an ass, but I shouldn't have been shocked when she countered—

"Actually, I would. The most important would be to keep things professional."

Two can play this game. "The next would be to make sure you do your job. Any more?"

"No one here can ever know we've had sex."

"I won't argue about that. So, that's it?"

She twisted her mouth to the side, and I couldn't help but imagine those juicy ass lips wrapped around my dick. "That's it."

"Well then, welcome to the Nelly's 101 empire, Ms. Kookman. It's a *pleasure* to have you."

She rolled her eyes. There's my Kookie. "The pleasure is all mine, Mr. Jacobs."

New rules are now in place.
Read their full length FWB to Lovers Romance in With Kookies on Top.

Afterword

Surprise! Though this novella is complete as their vacation fling story, it was only an introduction to Nelly and Yadah's future love story. This is how it started, but there's so much more to experience in their full novel!

Please do not forget to leave a review on Amazon and/or Goodreads for this book!

I hope you have enjoyed them thus far and yes, I know you have questions — you're supposed to due to that 'epilogue'!

Get all the answers to your questions in With Kookies On Top.

You can also get more Nelly & Yadah behind the scenes content, future potential one shots and more, in the Patreon!

Afterword

Thank you!

Hey You!

I want to thank you for reading my book. Each of my book babies mean so much to me and I'm grateful for you reading it and hopefully falling in love with it.

If you enjoy this book, **I would really appreciate if you could leave me a review on Amazon and/or Goodreads.** I would love to get as much feedback as possible from my readers, and reviews really do make a difference.

I plan to read each and every one of them and would love to hear your thoughts.

Thanks so much!

~ Bella Jay 🤍

Acknowledgments

I'm so happy to release another book! The feels never go away to be able to share new (or old) characters with you all! I hope you enjoyed Yadah and Nelly!

As always, thank you to everyone that continues to encourage and inspire me as a writer. You've all have helped me to continue to hone my craft and I'm thankful!

Thank you to my cover creator, AP! I love it so much and it gives me exactly what I needed it to give! Like this melanin!!

Thank you to my alpha / beta readers: Skye Moon, Meko, Tiff & Tessa! I value your thoughts and feedback more than you may think.

Thank you to my editors Hopeful Heartbreakers! Y'all came through per usual!

Thank you to anyone who has helped me and/or supported me in any way, big or small. I truly appreciate you more than you know.

Thank you in advance to every person who purchases, reads, reviews, and/or shares any of my book babies. I am appreciative of everyone!

Peace. Love. Write.

By Bella Jay

Standalones

Power [Jolee x Amare]

Holidaze [Nola x Bricks]

Here Comes The Sun [Bee x Mari]

Bookmarked [Books x Juice]

12:01 [Tyme x Midnight]

Jacobs Brothers Series

Finding Kristmas [Deuce + X]

Kookie Dough [Nelly + Yadah]

With Kookies on Top [Nelly + Yadah]

Four Letter Word Series

A Little Bit of Love - A Real Kind of Love Prequel [Ave + Siah]

A Real Kind of Love [Ave + Siah]

A Toxic Kind of Love [Addie + Landon]

A Selfish Kind of Love [Tessah + Kyree]

The Ways of Love [Addie + Waze]

*Each book in the FLW Series is a standalone but the books are meant to be read in order as the first three books take place during the same time. Book four, The Ways of Love takes place a year after the first three. If nothing else, it is **highly** recommended to read book two, A Toxic Kind of Love prior to The Ways of Love.*

Nobody But You Series (Collab with Skye Moon)

Completed Series Books 1 - 3

Holiday Dare Series

Mistletoe Blues [Joie + Blue]

Holiday Reads

Finding Kristmas

Holidaze

Mistletoe Blues

For my most updated catalog in order of release, please visit my website or scan the code: www.authorbellajay.com

BELLA JAY CATALOG

About the Author

Miami bred, Bella Jay (born Precious Rodgers) has had a love for books since she was a little girl. Getting lost in them was a favorite past time but writing them has become a true love. In 2018, with a little push she stepped out on faith and released her first novel to the world allowing her writer alter ego, Bella Jay, to take flight into the writing industry.

She writes spicy & contemporary Black love and romance books with unapologetically flawed characters who she loves to fix.

When she's not wrapped up in her characters, she can be found traveling the world, building her empire, sipping on tea or wine while reading a book, and wishing healthy eats were pancakes or cupcakes.

Website: www.authorbellajay.com

facebook.com/authorbellajay

tiktok.com/@authorbellajay

x.com/authorbellajay

instagram.com/authorbellajay

pinterest.com/authorbellajay

patreon.com/authorbellajay

www.ingramcontent.com/pod-product-compliance
Lightning Source LLC
Chambersburg PA
CBHW020652010826
48969CB00012B/822